ASSASSIN'S PREY

Assassins 2

Ella Sheridan

Also by Ella Sheridan

Assassins
The Assassin
Assassin's Mark
Assassin's Prey
Assassin's Heart
Assassin's Game

Southern Nights
Teach Me
Trust Me
Take Me

Southern Nights: Enigma
Come For Me
Deceive Me
Destroy Me
Deny Me

If Only
Only for the Weekend
Only for the Night
Only for the Moment

Secrets
Unavailable
Undisclosed
Unshakable

Want exciting extras from the ASSASSINS series? How about free book opportunities and bonus scenes? They're available only through my newsletter.
Sign up at ellasheridanauthor.com to get exclusive access!

Copyright

Assassins: Assassin's Mark
Copyright © 2018 Ella Sheridan

Cover Artist: Mayhem Cover Creations
Published in the United States.

Dedication

To Levi—

Life's rough and then you die. I can hear you saying that. And yet, here we are. I told you you'd get your happy ending whether you wanted it or not, didn't I?

You're not the one ultimately in control around here, brother.

Acknowledgments

To my awesome Prey beta team, Mary, Erika, and Kelly—thank you just doesn't quite cut it. You ladies are fantastic! I'm proud to call you my friends, a far more important designation than reader. Thank you, thank you, thank you!

And to my two best friends, my sister Dani Wade, and my daughter. I couldn't make it through this life without the two of you. Love you both so much!

Praise for the Assassins Series

"*Assassin's Mark* is an entertaining, fast-paced, with twists and turns that will keep you on your toes. Seriously, my Kindle was smoking!"
— *Anna's Bookshelf*

"Levi and Abby's story is suspenseful, and steamy! They share a sizzling chemistry."
— *Audiobook Fascination*

"With danger and steam and family and scheming, Assassin's Mark was pretty addictive. Ella Sheridan is onto the start of something good with this series." — Brittany's Book Blog

"Holy hotness Batman, this book could leave scorch marks!"
— *GA Book LoverX*

"OH MY EVERLOVIN HELL! This book was so exciting & kept me on the edge of my seat! There are big twists throughout, which had me dropping loud f-bombs throughout, all the way up to the end"
— *Power of Three Readers*

Chapter One

The silken sheets caressed her skin, revealing more than they concealed. Too damn much for my peace of mind. I should be out there, on the hunt, but Abby tethered me to her like a fucking chain, refusing to let go. No matter how much safer she was without me.

A gasp escaped her, and she turned on her side, one hand reaching out, searching—for me. "Levi?"

The room was dark, her eyes glazed with sleep. She couldn't see me in the shadows. It was better that way, but I couldn't leave her searching. Something inside me, something I both hated and hungered for, held as tightly to her as she did to me.

With a curse I couldn't quite hold back, I moved to the bed. And felt it the minute she saw me—my body lit up like I'd touched a live wire. Just like it did when prey appeared, every instinct sparking, every sense zeroed in on the body before me. Only I didn't want to kill this one.

I wanted her life in my hands, not her death.

A smile touched her full lips when my knee settled on the bed. Sheets rustled as she shifted onto her back, tugging me closer with nothing more than her creamy skin and the curve of her mouth. "There you are." The curve slowly flattened. "You're dressed."

Because it's safer this way. Because I can't sleep beside you and not let you all the way inside me.

I grabbed my T-shirt at the back of my neck and pulled. "Not for long."

I stripped as I crawled onto the bed. Crouching over Abby's body, I let the hunger for her take over, felt it in the tensing of my muscles, the lengthening of my cock, the racing of my heartbeat. A visceral reaction I was addicted to. That's all it was. She was my drug, and I'd never get enough. Not till it killed me. I just had to make sure it didn't kill her first.

"You should be asleep, little bird," I growled down at her.

Her eyes left mine, focused somewhere over my shoulder. Telling me all I needed to know. Another nightmare. Less frequent now, but they'd never go away. I knew that from personal experience.

"I never sleep as well when you're not beside me."

Another link clicked onto my chain, choking me with the need to reassure her. *I'll always be here. I need you beside me to sleep at all. I crave your skin against mine until I sometimes think I'll go insane.*

I didn't say any of it. I couldn't. The risk was too high.

So I kissed her.

Abby opened to me, a needy flower, defenseless, so fucking innocent even now. I remembered the first time I'd taken her, the first time she'd let me inside, and a groan escaped into her mouth. Her tight fit, the resistance I'd had to force myself through... Just the memory broke me out in a sweat.

I should hate myself for corrupting her. I did hate myself. But it felt more like she'd corrupted me.

With her sweetness, her fire. It made me weak when I couldn't afford to be. But I couldn't break free either.

Forcing myself back onto my knees, I fisted the sheet and pulled. A slow reveal—nipples, belly, that strip of auburn hair that pointed me straight to the entrance of her body. As if I could ever lose my way. The thought tightened the chain again, choking off my breath.

And then I looked into her eyes. Knowledge glittered there, too much for her own good. Every day it grew; every day she looked at me and that damn knowing was there. She knew my fear, but she never asked for more than I'd already given. Never asked for a commitment. Or if I loved her. As if she knew a yes would damn us both.

For the longest moment I wavered there, on the edge of leaving, fighting the bastard inside me that insisted I stay, the sight of her laid out before me searing my brain. And then Abby shifted, her legs parting, and the scent of her need filled my nose. The balance tipped. An agonized groan rumbled from my brain to my chest and out of my mouth.

I was between her legs before my next heartbeat.

Cream and spice, that was Abby on my tongue. I pressed my mouth to her pussy and pushed deep, seeking out every drop. Filling my senses with her until I knew I was drowning. Her skin was slick velvet against my lips, my tongue, her clit a hard bead against my nose. I licked up, took it into my mouth, and sucked hard, that primal need to nurse, to take my nourishment from her, hitting me like a bullet to the chest. She filled me, sustained me—with her body, her desire, the hungry cries echoing in my ears, the greedy fingers forcing my head closer. Her body and her mouth begged me for more, and I gave it, again and again and again until she exploded beneath my tongue.

I was inside her before the last ripple faded.

"Levi, God, yes!"

My cock was so heavy, so tight inside her hot, wet body. Too much. Not enough. When her seeking hands landed on my chest and slid downward, I knew this would be over before it had a chance to begin, and no way in hell could I allow that.

"No." Her wrists were fragile in my rough hands, but I forced them back anyway, slamming them to the bed as Abby cried out beneath me. "Look at me, little bird. Now."

Frantic, pleading hazel eyes snapped to mine. Abby rolled her pelvis, taking me deeper. "Please."

"Look at me," I demanded. "Don't close your eyes."

I pulled back, the drag of her body around my cock so perfect my eyes threatened to roll back in my head. Leveraging my knees out, I slammed back inside. Abby gasped my name, and I did it again. And again. Those beautiful eyes glazed over, going somewhere deep inside herself where hunger and pleasure roared for satisfaction, taking me with her. Letting me see what no one else had ever seen— Abby, bare, open, completely vulnerable. To me. Alive like no one I'd ever known before, filling and feeding the dead parts of me that I'd long ago given up hope of ever healing.

She could; she did. With her body and her honesty.

I'd never met anyone like her before. And I knew it was only a matter of time before I destroyed her.

Without warning her eyes flared, her legs bending to hook around my hips, pulling me closer. She chanted my name, high and desperate, and I angled my hips up, the head of my cock striking that spot deep inside that made her clench around me, so tight I had to force my way back in. And I did.

My name morphed into a scream on her lips as she climaxed around me. Squeezed me tight and sucked every last drop of semen from my willing body.

The relaxing of her muscles beneath mine drew me out of the fog of pleasure a few minutes later. I raised my head from her neck, glanced down. Abby blinked, her expression smoothing out, but not before I caught a glimpse of the emotions there—longing, desperation, pain. My failure, all in one look. But it was how it had to be.

"I have to go."

Before she could respond, I was up and headed to the bathroom. I cleaned myself up, wiping away the evidence of her pleasure and mine, thankful that with Abby's birth control, condoms were no longer an issue. I could be skin to skin with her, mark her, smear my semen over her body so that no other man would dare to trespass on my territory. I needed it. The animal inside me needed it, demanded it. With her I could soothe the savage hunger.

But no kids. Ever.

I returned to the bed with a warm washcloth. Abby parted her legs willingly. When she was clean, I leaned down until my nose met her pubic hair, and breathed deep. *My Abby. My woman!* the animal inside me roared. But the man restricted me to a brief kiss on her sensitive clit before backing away.

Abby's murmur of disappointment was a knife to the gut.

"I'll lock up before I leave," I told her.

She lay, silent, on the bed, legs bent, body gleaming in the faint light from the crack in the curtains, and watched me return the cloth to the bathroom. With every piece of clothing I added to my body, the silence became sharper, carving me up with its accusing edge.

I moved quickly to check the windows, then walked to the door. I'd melted into the shadows before I heard her voice. "What about a kiss goodbye?"

I couldn't deny her, not when my body screamed for the kiss too. I returned to the bed, let the covers caress her skin once again as I drew them over her. "Sleep, little bird."

Her kiss was the padlock on the chain that held me to her. I welcomed it in that moment—delved deep to tangle with her tongue, nipped her lips, buried my face in the hollow of her neck and the sweet scent of vanilla and flowers.

"Be safe," she murmured as I backed away.

"Always."

And then I was out the door. Every window, every door was checked, secured—I wouldn't risk anything happening when I wasn't here. The shadows in the backyard were deep this time of night, but unmoving. Same on either side of the house. When I walked out the front door and set the security system to on, I did so knowing she was safe inside.

So why did my soul scream at me to go back with every step I took away from her?

Chapter Two

"The fucker will back off if he knows what's good for him," I growled into my earpiece. The words were low enough that the crowds on the sidewalk couldn't hear the specifics, but they didn't need to. They created a wide berth around me from no more than a glance. I preferred it that way.

"He'll back off, bro. No worries." Eli chuckled in my ear. "Your reputation precedes you."

It better. I'd built the fear of reprisal into my business model, and very few risked stepping over the line and triggering it. But this latest contract…

It reminded me too much of Abby's father. And that reminded me too much of Remi being shot, having a gun pointed at Abby's head. The memories could—and did—send me into a rage.

Councilman Roslyn was dead and gone; I tried to remember that. But my body's visceral reaction had me throwing off angry waves the people around me couldn't miss.

My brothers and Abby were the only ones who knew the full story of Roslyn's involvement with, as he would have put it, the unsavory but necessary elements of society. We kept that secret for her safety, not mine. If it had been public, I wouldn't be dealing with the fucking asshat I was now. But I wouldn't risk her by tying her to me. She would never be touched by my life.

I'd made that mistake once. Never again.

My current client, however...he would be touched, all right. And I'd take great satisfaction in doing the touching. And breaking. Two days since I'd seen Abby, *two days*—because this latest contract had been a major fuckup.

"Tell me about this meeting," I barked, still seething as I turned the corner at Holmes and Sanderson and headed farther into downtown.

"Abby's lawyer, Lance Heinz, called," Eli told me. "Seems the forensic accountant was able to uncover some more accounts linked to her father. In order to retrieve the money, they need some signatures and shit. Remi knows the details."

I could hear the shrug in my youngest brother's voice, ratcheting up my tension. Remi was with Abby, not me. I knew he'd protect her with his life, but I didn't want him to. I didn't want any of them in danger. I needed to be at her side, not fucking walking down the sidewalk like I was taking a Sunday stroll. Not that anyone around me could call it *strolling*. More like a bull chasing down a matador.

Which totally worked for me.

Even without the delay, it made sense for Remi to be with her for the meeting at First Bank and Trust. He was a genius when it came to accounting. Not that anyone there would realize it. To the outside world we were her bodyguards. No one knew our true faces—I'd gone to great lengths to keep it that way—so we could safely travel with her, keep her protected, on the rare occasions she had to deal with anything concerning her father.

"Have you got the camera feeds live?" I asked.

Eli's snort drilled into my ear. "Are you really asking me that?"

Yes, because I was a micromanaging bastard. Knowing that didn't stop me from doing it. "Are they?"

"Of course they fucking are. I've got two screens with every traffic camera in a five-block radius. I've tapped into private security feeds, including at the business across the street from the parking garage you demanded Remi use. Nice scowl, by the way. I can also tell you that Remi and Abby are two blocks up on your left, approaching the cross street a block ahead of the light at Sanderson and First Street. Better get a move on, bro."

The intersection where the bank was located was three blocks north of my current location. I broke into a slow jog, my brain automatically scanning, assessing, countering. Traffic, pedestrians, cameras. The crisp fall breeze pushed people along the street, so no one lingered. No hint of a threat arose. Perfect.

The phone in my pocket vibrated against my hip—a text, not a call. I reached for it, glancing at the display. Remi.

Crossing street now.

My nerves went tight. Only two blocks away. I picked up speed as the intersection where Remi would be escorting Abby came into view. There, on the opposite side of the road. The bright red dress coat Abby wore stood out like a beacon, a stark contrast to her auburn hair.

I cursed under my breath. Apparently not low enough, because an older woman passing me skittered to the side at my vicious "fuck." I ignored her recoil and kept going.

Abby and Remi were the only ones at the crosswalk. I knew when the walk light flipped on;

they stepped into the street in front of the rows of stopped cars. My brother's tall, heavy frame dwarfed Abby as he took her arm, staying on the side of oncoming traffic. Everything seemed normal, nothing to worry about. So why did my every instinct scream at me to get them both out of sight?

The loud whine of a motorcycle engine hit my ears.

I glanced back. A sleek black Yamaha shot through the stopped cars, straddling the line as it zoomed forward. I had just enough time to notice the driver—black leather, black helmet, tinted visor that gave nothing away—before he passed me.

Headed straight for the crosswalk. At full speed.

"Abby!"

Remi's head jerked around at my shout. Realization struck, widening his eyes. He grabbed Abby around the waist and ran for the sidewalk—just as the rider drew a gun.

Time stopped. I could see the glint of the sun on the metal barrel. See the leather-gloved finger on the trigger. Remi's eyes went wild, and he launched himself toward the thick, ancient oak waiting next to the street, the only thing that could possibly protect them against a bullet at point-blank range. He and Abby flew through the air as the gun came up.

"Fuck, fuck, fuck!" My hand went to my chest, to the holster beneath my suit jacket, as I sprinted toward them. I'd never make it in time. My heart knew that and roared with impotent rage.

My woman. *Mine.*

Too far.

Between one heartbeat and the next, Remi and Abby hit the ground and rolled, Remi twisting their bodies behind the massive trunk of the tree.

The ping of silenced gunshots—one, two, three—reached my ears a second later. The motorcycle accelerated through the intersection, barely missing a hit from an oncoming semi.

And then it was gone.

I rushed to Abby's side.

"What the fuck?" Remi yelled.

I grasped the lapels of Abby's coat with shaking hands, cursing my own weakness but unable to stop the reaction, and pulled her to sitting. "Late model bike, no plates, no distinguishing marks, driver unknown," I told him, keeping my voice low. Maybe we could get something on the traffic cameras, but I didn't think so. Our man was a professional.

The job I could do. It was handling my woman that was killing me. She was breathing fast and shallow, her eyes dilated with fear. Tremors racked her slender body. "Abby?"

She grabbed on to my coat just as hard as I had her. "I'm okay."

A quick survey showed no visible cuts or bruises, though I knew the latter would show up eventually. She buried her head against me and shook.

A crowd had started to gather. "Let's go."

"But Remi—"

Abby turned to my brother, but he was already up and flanking her. He knew exactly what I did—we had to get her out of here, now. This had been a setup.

"Let's go," I repeated, half carrying and half dragging her through the people circling us. "Now."

She could fall apart later. Right now, safety came before feelings.

Abby knew the tone I used. She was no longer the girl I'd been able to frighten into compliance, but she was smart; she knew when to obey. Her feet stumbled but caught up to my pace, and she held her tongue as Remi and I hurried her down the block, away from the bank.

"Car?" I asked Remi.

"I'll get it." He jerked his chin down the block toward the garage on the other side of the street.

"Eli?" I barked.

My earpiece crackled back to life. "I've got him covered." He'd watch Remi's back from surrounding cameras.

Remi already had his keys out. "Let's go, little brother," he told Eli.

I knew one of them would text me where to meet. In the meantime I wanted Abby out of sight. We hurried down the block, then took a left on the cross street where Remi took a right. A coffee shop waited just ahead. As we stepped inside, I scanned the line, tables, staff. Nothing set my warning buzzers off. I hustled Abby across the room and into a bathroom at the back, making sure to lock the door behind me.

"What are we—"

My mouth on hers ate up the rest of her words. Noise galloped in my ears, drowning out everything but the agony of knowing I'd almost lost her. Lost this. She opened to me just like I needed her to, let me claim her. It wasn't until the taste of salt registered on my tongue that I was able to leash the savage intensity driving me and pull back.

"Shh." I eased away, my fingers automatically wiping at the tears running down her ghost-white cheeks. "You're okay. Everything's okay, little bird."

She laughed, a sickly little sound that ended in a hiccup. "Just reaction. I'll stop soon, I promise."

I hated tears. They were a distraction, a weakness, sometimes a weapon. But I'd learned enough with Abby to know she sometimes had to let it out. She got from tears what I got from sex or a fight—a release.

I hugged her closer, burying her face in my neck, trying hard to ignore the blood pooling in my groin. With Abby in the same room, much less against me, the reaction was a given; with the adrenaline roaring through my system, it was raging-caveman aggressive. I needed to fuck her, reassure us both that we were alive, that she was safe.

Abby didn't need to deal with that shit right now. Later...

Slowly the shudders in her body quieted. I gave her a minute more, then leaned my upper body back so I could look into her eyes. "Okay."

She sucked in a massive breath. "Okay."

I shucked my coat. "Let's get you cleaned up."

Abby removed her coat and blouse at my urging. While she splashed cold water over her face, I took off my button-down. It would be big on her, but what mattered was the color, not the fit. After drying her face, I buttoned her into it.

"I think you might draw more attention than me with that look," she said, eyeing my bare chest, the expanse of tattoos marking my body. And fuck if that look didn't have my cock tighter than a drum. She'd always been fascinated by my ink.

"No doubt." I shrugged back into my sport coat. Buttoned, only a vee of skin at the collar showed. Abby's coat I turned inside out before holding it for her to slide on. "Want the shirt?"

She glanced at her blouse, bunched in my fist. Another shudder shook her. "No."

I tossed it in the trash can just as my phone buzzed in my pocket.

"Remi's ready. Let's go."

Chapter Three

"I'm not going into hiding and that's final!" Abby shouted. "I didn't build a whole new life so some stranger can waltz in and steal it away from me."

"It would just be until we figure out what's going on," Eli said, much more mildly than I could at the moment. All my fury at almost having my woman killed in front of me had found a new target at her refusal to lay low. If my teeth hadn't been clenched so hard I thought a few of them would crack any minute, I'd definitely say something I'd regret later.

Like *I kidnapped you once. Don't make me do it again.*

Yeah, that would go over like a bullet to the gut. A nice, slow, agonizingly painful death.

The stubborn set to Abby's jaw didn't soften. "No."

The need to force her hitched my step as I paced across the room. A warehouse, not unlike the one I'd first brought her to over a year ago. I had a string of safe houses in and around the city, but this was our new base of operations. It was probably good that the floor and walls of this one were cement, or I'd be punching my way through them right about now.

Leaving Abby's refusal for later, I turned my attention to this afternoon's attack. "What have we got so far?" I asked Remi.

He glanced up from the bank of computers where both my brothers sat. "Definitely a professional. I traced the bike through traffic cameras as far as I could, but it disappeared about four miles down the road."

So the driver knew where cameras could track him. Too much knowledge for someone without resources—or a backup team. This had been planned in advance.

"What about the accounts?"

Eli swiveled his computer chair to face me. "Nothing yet. I'm not sure if it's the accountant or the lawyer, but I'll find out."

Someone had set Abby up; it was just a matter of tracking down who. "Or it was neither and they were set up too."

Eli grunted. "Exactly. I'm working on hacking as we speak. If there's anything in their e-mails or bank accounts, I'll uncover it. It'll just take a little time."

Time we didn't have, not if Abby was the target. One second was too long to let that shit stand.

"Remi, see what you can dig up, either online or on the streets. If someone is moving into our territory, they can't do it silently. Someone will know. These guys have to have been brought in from the outside. No one here is organized enough for this, much less has the balls to cross us. Not after—"

Remi's gaze cut to Abby, and I shut my mouth. She didn't need another reminder of her bastard of a father.

"The question is," Eli said, ignoring the byplay, "who brought them in. And why now? Why Abby?"

"We'll find out," Remi said.

Now that both men knew where to concentrate, I turned to my woman. I could see her shoulders tighten, knew she was prepared to fight. The thought excited me as much as it angered me, the sick, volatile mix swirling in my gut. I stalked toward her.

"Levi—"

Not with an audience. Grasping her arm, I kept walking. Abby tried to resist, but we were in the bedroom with the door closed before I let her go.

She glared up at me, the fire in her eyes fanning the flames in my body. "You can't force me to stay here."

One eyebrow went up. Abby swallowed hard, and God help me, but satisfaction made my cock swell even more.

"Look at you." She scoffed despite not being able to meet my eyes. "You act like a peacock, puffing up to intimidate his mate, but I'm not a bird, no matter what you call me. I'm a woman with a life. A life that matters, Levi."

"I never said it didn't."

"No, you just act like it."

Because I had to. There was no use arguing over it.

"I've... I just started classes. I—" She drew her bottom lip in, nibbling on it. "I'm getting somewhere, can't you see that? Don't derail me now."

I wasn't the one responsible. The man, woman, group, whoever it was who'd targeted her—they were the ones to blame. That didn't stop the guilt that rose as I stared into her pleading hazel eyes.

And this was the problem with us, right here. The only consideration should be her safety, not her feelings. Hurting her felt like stabbing myself, but I was used to pain—I hardened my heart and plowed on. "Anywhere you would go, routines, patterns, anything that could be tracked online is a way to find you. To hurt you."

"Then my school, my home, my car—all those records lead right back to me. I can't avoid them and still have a life."

"No, you can't." That's exactly why I lived the way I did. Why my brothers had no life, as she so succinctly put it. Because it was dangerous.

After her father's death last year, I'd left Abby alone, thinking it was better for her to have her freedom. She was just getting started when the hunger became too much, when I couldn't breathe another second without her, and I'd shown up on her doorstep, dragging her right back into my world like the selfish bastard that I was. I'd regretted that for the last three months.

But after today, after seeing her targeted and knowing there was no way for her to protect herself? I'd get down on my knees and thank God for making me a fucking asshole if I believed in him anymore. I hadn't been able to protect my parents, but my brothers and Abby? I'd do it or die trying. Even if she hated my guts for a little while.

"I won't give up everything I've worked so hard for because some dickhead has decided to target me for whatever reason," Abby said.

Frustration turned her creamy skin a pale pink that made me want to run my tongue over it, see if she was as hot as she looked—and tasted as good. I let the need spark in my own eyes, throwing Abby off her game.

Her gaze dropped to my shoulder, but she didn't give up. "Why can't you just protect me at my place?"

"Because I have a job too, and I can't be on top of you twenty-four-seven."

She squirmed, and I knew my words had sent her mind in other directions besides leaving. Good. A solid hour in bed would help work out the frustration coiling me as tight as a drum.

Abby wasn't that easily swayed, though. Stubborn to a fault, she strode for the door. "I'm not staying, Levi. That's final."

I stepped into her path, blocking the door, and folded my arms over my chest.

"Move," she barked.

My blank stare answered for me, and Abby's color heightened even more. She was pissed; I got that. But I wasn't letting her leave. If she needed to take out her frustration, scream, yell, hit me...whatever. I could take it. But I wasn't budging from this spot.

But she didn't strike out. She threw her head back, fists white with tension, her angry growl ripping through the air, but it didn't rock the warehouse. And when she lowered her head and met my eyes again, it wasn't only anger in them. The surface roiled with it, but underneath, there was something else, something that set me on alert. A bomb was coming my way, and I braced for it the only way I knew how.

By tightening down even further.

"I can't..." She squeezed her eyes shut. Blinked them open. "I can't do this anymore, Levi."

My breath caught in my throat, choking me. "What the hell are you talking about?" Because no fucking way did she mean what I thought she meant.

"This." Her anger filtered away as she waved a hand between us. That something under the surface shot to the top—grief. "It hurts too much."

I was giving her everything I had to give. That shouldn't hurt. It should be enough. *I* should be enough.

"I can't keep getting drawn into your world, Levi. The uncertainty. The instability. I can't live without a life, without something that belongs to me."

"I belong to you." As much as I could belong to anyone. I'd given up fighting that after staying away from her for a year and nearly going insane.

She blinked, and a tear rolled down her heated cheek. "Do you?" She gave that little laugh/hiccup sound that had nothing to do with amusement. "You can't even sleep with me. You fuck me and you wait till I'm asleep—if I'm lucky—and then you're gone. You're a ghost that visits when you want sex and hides from me when you don't. I can't live like this anymore. I need all of you."

"All of me isn't available to give, Abby." The words might seem ugly, brutal even, but they were the truth. And that was the only thing I could give her. The only thing I was fully capable of giving.

I didn't believe there was an *all* when it came to me. *All* had been chopped into tiny little pieces by life, scattered and lost, hardened and honed by death, and I couldn't be put back together again. It wasn't possible. If it had been, I'd have done it for Abby a long time ago.

Her fist came up to press hard over her heart. She closed her eyes, and I could see her mentally trying to pull herself together. To re-form the shell that protected her from hurt. From me.

The animal deep inside roared a denial.

"I can't," she finally whispered, the words as broken as she looked. "I can't be with you, Levi."

The animal tore free. "You damn well can," I shouted, stalking toward her.

Abby backed up, her shoulders hitting the concrete wall. "Why? So I can lie there at night and watch you walk out the door? Why is it so easy for you to leave me? And I can't do the same?"

She thought it was easy? When it felt like tearing my guts out every time? But the pain was worth it if it kept her safe. It wasn't easy; it was necessary.

I gripped her arms, my fingers biting into her flesh harder than they should, but I couldn't stop them. Couldn't stop the heartbeat banging in my throat and the blood pooling low in my gut, screaming at me to subdue her, take her, force her to see that she would never walk out of my life. "You're not leaving. You're staying with me until we get this shit figured out. You're going to be safe."

"My body, maybe. You've already destroyed my heart."

The words pierced me, the stabbing pain making me want to curl up and protect my vulnerable underbelly. Too late. She'd already gutted me.

"I won't leave my life behind to skulk in the shadows, waiting around for you to notice me," she was saying.

I barked a laugh through the agony ripping me apart. "You breathe and I notice you. I can't stop noticing you. I take one look and my dick is rock-hard and my entire body hones in on one thing: you. Getting you beneath me." I shook her as if it was her fault, because it was. All her fault. "I can't breathe for wanting you." One step and our bodies came together. Her nipples were hard, poking through the cotton of her bra and my dress shirt. She didn't want to leave any more than I wanted her to.

Abby licked her lips, turned her head away from me. "I'm not talking about sex."

"I am." It was all I knew. The only way to share myself with her. And right now I needed it just as much as I needed my next lungful of air.

The kiss I took then didn't feel like love. It felt like conquering. Overpowering. I pried her lips open with my own, and when my tongue invaded her mouth, she shuddered—not with fear or pain, but with need. I knew because her teeth unclenched and she let me in, a whimper of defeat echoing between our lips. I plundered and invaded, every crack and crevice, until her head was bent back like a broken reed and her eyes were dazed with hunger. Only then did I bury my face in the hollow of her neck. When I bit down on her shoulder, she startled against me.

"You're not leaving," I growled around her flesh.

"Yes, I am."

I nipped the tender line of her shoulder, my fingers tightening on her once more—a threat, a promise. "No, you're not. You're coming with me."

She shook her head as much as she could with my face in the way, my teeth gliding along her skin. "Whether I want to or not? For how long, Levi?"

Forever. "For as long as I say."

That sick little chuckle again. "And what about what I say?"

"Doesn't matter." I could change what she said, whether she chose to acknowledge that fact or not. We both knew it.

I felt her inhale, readying to fight me again. Her chance was cut off by a knock on the door.

I stepped back and stared her down. "Come."

The door opened. The steps hesitated before moving around to where I could see the intruder. Remi.

"Sorry to interrupt, but there's a development you need to know about."

Nothing could be as important as the battle of wills going on right here in this bedroom. The battle for the future. "What?" I barked.

"Lance Heinz is dead."

And God help me, but satisfaction settled low in my gut even as the last bit of light died out of Abby's soulful eyes.

Chapter Four

She reminded me of a wounded kitten every time I looked at her. Like I'd threatened to step on her with my big bad boots instead of fighting for her life, for us, the only way I knew how.

With Heinz's death, at least she couldn't argue about safety. She'd agreed to stay with us for a few days, which was why she was upstairs right now, packing a suitcase while I prowled through the downstairs rooms of her house. I wouldn't go up there. If I did, I'd fuck her until she could do nothing but chant my name to the rhythm of my cock thrusting inside her, forgetting everything but me. Forgetting that she wanted to leave me.

That wouldn't get her to safety. But tonight, when I had her back at base? She'd learn her lesson.

And yet, with every glance, every step, hell, every inhale as I walked the darkened rooms, I found reason after reason why we shouldn't be together. Why I would ruin her life.

I truly was an animal, because I couldn't stop. Even now, soaking in the peace of the home she'd built for herself. A place where every corner smelled like vanilla and flowers, as if Abby had just walked by, her presence lingering around me. Every edge was softened with fabric and padding and care. So much fucking care. The colors were warm, the furniture deeply cushioned. The kind you sank into and never wanted to leave, with fluffy blankets over the backs that felt like silk against your skin. The kind normal men might cuddle under with their wife while she read a book and he watched the latest football game on the flat-screen TV. The kind my parents had taken the time to share on a cold winter's day.

Just like they'd shared a soft bed at night. And died together in it.

My skin crawled, a thousand ants scurrying over it. I bit out a "fuck" and paced into the kitchen.

Remi stood at the counter, his hand literally in the cookie jar. Abby even had a damn cookie jar.

"Get the fuck out of there."

Remi stuffed the cookie he held into his mouth, his other hand still digging for more. "Why?"

"Because it's not yours, asshole." And seeing my twenty-eight-year-old brother stealing cookies brought back even more ugly memories. Of another kitchen, another jar, and a dirt-smudged, towheaded boy stuffing his face. Why were the memories before my parents' murder so much more gut-wrenchingly painful than afterward?

"Hey, you got the girl," Remi mumbled around a mouthful. "The least we can get for risking our asses is oatmeal molasses cookies."

God, not the oatmeal ones. If I walked any closer, the scent of butter and molasses and brown sugar would overpower me, I knew. I couldn't admit a weakness for anything, including a goddamn cookie.

My vision went red. "Get your fucking hand out of the fucking jar, then get your fucking ass out on patrol before I put my steel-toed boot up it!"

Remi raised an eyebrow. "Don't get your panties in a twist."

I stepped closer.

With a slant to his lips that looked suspiciously like a pout, Remi grabbed a fistful of cookies, put the lid back on the jar, and headed for the garage. "Dickhead," he muttered under his breath.

"You're damn right," I called after him. Remi shot a bird over his shoulder—with the hand not full of cookies.

Fucking hell.

My watch said we'd been here ten minutes, which was ten minutes too long. Time to get the hell out of Dodge. Trying to roll some of the tension from my knotted shoulders, I pivoted, my target the stairs and Abby. I'd almost reached them when the sound of shattering glass took over my world.

Thousands of shards flew through the air. My arm came up automatically to protect my face, but not before the sting of a hundred scratches raced across my skin. A loud *whoosh* filled my ears, the sound duplicated behind me.

I lowered my arm in time to see the carpet runner lining the steps burst into flames. A Molotov cocktail. As I processed what I was seeing, a second bottle shot through the shattered window. A similar impact echoed in the living room.

"Damn it!"

Something happens to a man when he's used to battle, when fighting is his world. The adrenaline rush comes later. In the moment, everything slows—time, your breathing, your heart rate. All that exists is the calculations in your head, the plan. In that moment my focus went laser tight, my only thought whether I should hit those stairs running or not.

"Abby!" I crept as close to the stairs as the ball of flames would allow, the heat shriveling my skin. "Abby!"

Her face, pinched and white, appeared in the upstairs hallway. "Levi!"

Footsteps pounded the hardwood floor behind me. I pivoted and dropped to one knee, my gun coming up in a heartbeat.

"It's me." Remi advanced despite the gun in his face, brushing glass from his hair and shoulders.

"Garage too?" I asked.

A sharp nod answered me. Damn it. Both Abby's car and mine were in there. They could blow any minute. And if they went, so did the gas line in the kitchen.

"The French doors in the living room are toast," Remi said. "Looks like there's another down the hall. They got us on all four corners."

They wanted us to die. And if we didn't, if we got out, they would most likely be waiting.

Fuck. Fuck fuck fuck.

"Take the basement," I told Remi. We'd extended the space to include an escape tunnel that exited in the woods behind Abby's house. "Come around behind the bastards if you can, see what you can find. There'll be at least four of them."

He didn't wait. We both knew how critical time was. Already the smoke was obscuring my view of Abby at the top of the stairs, stinging my eyes, filling my lungs. Soon the heat would push her completely out of my sight.

"Abby!"

She peered around the corner again. Her eyes were wild, terrified, but she didn't back down. That was my woman.

"You can't get down the stairs," I yelled. There weren't any stairs any longer, not near me. Two Molotov cocktails could do a helluva lot of damage. "Go back to your room and out the window."

"That's a second-story window!"

"I know. I'll catch you, little bird. Now go!"

I'd always be there to catch her, whether she wanted me gone or not.

I waited long enough to see her dart back down the hallway before turning away from the fire. The dining room was to my back, far enough away that the flames hadn't touched it yet. Pulling my T-shirt up to cover my mouth, I hurried to the window overlooking the front lawn. My gun was still in my hand, at the ready, as I eased around the window casing to check the front yard. Neighbors were gathering in the cul-de-sac, pointing, shouting, some with cell phones to their ears. Good. A crowd was the best safety I could give Abby at the moment, probably the one thing our attackers hadn't counted on.

Tucking my gun away, I slid the window open and climbed out. Several men rushed in my direction.

"Are you all right?" one asked, reaching for my arm.

I kept myself rigid, kept my instinct to fight in check. These men were Abby's neighbors—I knew because we'd thoroughly vetted each and every one of them. They weren't our enemies here. "I'm fine." I coughed. "Abby's upstairs."

From the corner of my eye, I saw something fly through the air toward the ground. Abby's suitcase.

"Help!"

I rushed toward the opposite side of the house. "Abby! I'm here."

Her window was open, her head and upper body leaning over the sill. Smoke poured out around her.

"That flowerbed should cushion her fall," one of the men said as they surrounded me. The bed was mounded with mulch and big, green, leafy plants I didn't know the name of. The man was right, but I had no intention of letting Abby hit the ground. I'd catch her first.

"Abby, straddle the sill, then push your legs out," I yelled up. Sirens sounded in the distance, and I prayed that between the crowd and the firemen and Remi out there somewhere, it was enough to keep Abby safe from whoever had attacked. "Come on, little bird. I'll catch you."

I could see tear streaks in the smudges on her face. She was scared, but she did as I asked. I wanted to tear the men who'd done this apart with my bare hands.

A coughing fit seized Abby as she maneuvered into position. I watched, helpless and raging, as she dangled, her belly on the windowsill, coughing so hard I thought she'd choke.

The men around me called encouragement. I ignored them, sidling up until I stood directly beneath Abby's window. Putting every inch of command I had into my voice, I barked up at her. "Move it, Abby!"

She wiggled backward. "You'll catch me?"

"Always."

She slipped down farther until she hung by her grip on the windowsill. Maybe ten feet separated her from my arms.

A window somewhere in the house shattered, reminding me that the kitchen was likely on fire. We had to get away from here.

"Drop!" I yelled.

She let go.

The fall took forever and mere seconds. Pain shot through my arms and chest as her body hit me, sending me onto my ass. I rolled immediately to set Abby on the ground and scrambled to my feet. Between me and the group of men, we hustled her toward the street as the first fire truck pulled up.

Seconds later, the back portion of her house exploded. The pressure didn't reach us around front, but Abby hit her knees anyway. Choking sobs racked her body.

I stood to one side a few minutes later, watching a paramedic push an oxygen mask at Abby while another treated the scrapes on her hands and forearms where the brick had shaved off several layers of skin. The crowd still milled around, many of the women coming over to offer Abby help if she needed it. Offering sympathy. Caring. All I had to offer was safety, but I knew which one Abby would choose. Her eyes constantly sought me out, making sure I was nearby, making sure I was okay. My gaze was always waiting for hers.

She was alive. We were alive. When the paramedics finally let me close, I scooped her into my arms and buried my face in her smoke-scented hair.

That's when the adrenaline hit.

Chapter Five

The oxygen mask obscured most of Abby's face. The paramedics had tried to give me one too, but I'd shoved them off. I needed to be able to move, not tethered to a machine. Abby needed their attention, not me.

I'd held her for long moments, grounding us both, but my need to protect her had finally driven me to my feet. I kept my fingers wrapped around her nape as they treated a bump on her head where she'd connected with the brick during the fall. My gaze swept the crowd continually, watching for anyone who didn't belong, but with the fire department and EMTs and people streaming in from all over the neighborhood to check out the fire, it was impossible to tell if anyone was paying the wrong kind of attention.

Remi had briefly appeared in my line of sight. He and Eli were out there, watching, wary. I should be out there with them, on the hunt, finding the bastards who'd done this, but Abby was my first priority, always—even if I compromised my own safety for hers. It went against everything I'd taught myself, everything I'd taught my brothers, but I couldn't escape it, no matter how much my brain said I should. The rest of me told my brain to fuck off and stayed.

Two hits in twenty-four hours. There was no fast escape this time, but my brothers would watch our backs until I could get Abby away.

The paramedic finally stepped back, and that was when the cops moved in. Partners, apparently, one older and one not, both in the detectives' uniform of cheap slacks and uncomfortable sport coats. "Ma'am," the older one said, his focus on Abby.

I felt the muscles in her neck tighten, her spine straighten. She more than anyone knew how carefully I avoided official attention, but there was no choice here: I wouldn't leave her alone. If that meant records, well, we could always erase them later.

"I'm Detective Bryant. We'd like to get a statement if you're able."

A shock ran through me as I stared at the guy. Gray hair, gruff voice—I knew that voice. Knew him. The knowledge burst through me with a nausea chaser. He might be nineteen years older and have more lines on his face, more weight sagging over his belt, but I'd never forget that voice. Detective Bryant had worked my parents' murder case.

Fuck.

Abby pulled the oxygen mask off. "I'm fine." The gravel of her words clearly said she wasn't, but no one argued with her. I couldn't resist running my thumb along her pulse, though. When had reassuring her become vital?

About twenty-four hours after I'd met her, probably. No matter how much my jackass self had fought it.

The cop's gaze dropped to my thumb, then rose to me. His eyes narrowed—trying to figure out why I seemed familiar? All he needed was my name, and he'd have it soon enough; they'd want ID, and I didn't have an alternate on me. So Levi it was.

I shifted against the rear door of the ambulance, all too aware of the handgun tucked in the small of my back.

"Your name?" he asked Abby.

She gave her name and other pertinent information, both of us watching as the younger officer wrote everything down. When it came time to explain what had happened, Abby swallowed hard.

"I don't know for certain." She shrugged, her injuries emphasizing the helpless look in her eyes. "I was upstairs when it started. I heard windows breaking, then the fire…" Her swallow pushed against my thumb. "I got out through my bedroom window."

"And where were you, sir?" Bryant asked.

"Downstairs."

"Your name?"

My gut clenched. "Levi Agozi."

The man's narrowed eyes went wide. "Agozi?"

From the corner of my eye I caught Abby glancing between us, concern tightening her features. I squeezed her nape gently, reassuring her even as I held Bryant's gaze. "Yes."

"Your parents were Miriam and Nathaniel Agozi."

It wasn't a question, and I didn't answer. Bryant shifted to meet his partner's eyes. "Double homicide years ago. We never caught the perp," he said. Turned back to me. "Your uncle sent you to a boarding school, if I recall correctly. You and your brothers."

Wrong. But then if Amos Agozi had let it be known that we'd run away, my uncle wouldn't have been able to keep questions at bay—and he'd desperately needed to. I shrugged. "Our guardian wasn't big on children."

Bryant grunted, not seeming surprised.

"And the two of you are…" He glanced between Abby and me.

"Levi's my b-boyfriend."

She'd never used that word with me. What we had was far deeper, more intense than boyfriend/girlfriend. I wasn't a boy, for one. I was a killer. And I should be hunting right now, not dragging up the past.

Abby shuddered under my hand. I glanced down, met the uncertainty in her eyes. A corner of my mouth turned up without conscious thought, giving her the reassurance she craved. She leaned toward me, her shoulder, then forehead hitting my hip.

"I'd really like to get her home as soon as possible, gentlemen," I told Bryant. "As you can see, it's been a night, and there'll be a lot of work ahead of us in the next few days."

Bryant kept glancing between the two of us, a vee digging grooves between his brows. "Of course. Please tell us what you witnessed."

I did as succinctly as possible.

"Ms. Roslyn, who would be targeting you like this?"

Abby huffed a laugh, shaking her head so that it rolled against me. "I have no clue. As you are aware, I'm sure, there were issues a while ago with my father. Since then, nothing."

Good girl. Mentioning the incident earlier today would only bring more scrutiny. We couldn't cover the way the fire had started, but there was no need to draw the police in with more suspicion. Bryant was already too focused on me as it was.

"I live here quietly, no issues, good neighbors." Abby's eyes glazed with tears. "Normal."

Her voice choked on the last word, hitting me like a throat punch. *Normal.* I could never give her normal.

"We'll be talking to the fire investigator, see what we can find out, but we'll need to speak to you again, try to nail down what might have caused someone to do this," Bryant said. "We have your contact information. If you are available, we'd like to reinterview you in the next couple of days, see if anything new comes to mind."

Abby nodded, keeping her chin down, her auburn hair veiling her face. "Of course."

"You have my number," I said, pulling their attention from her. "Call anytime."

The men nodded, turned to leave. I couldn't miss the way Bryant glanced over his shoulder as they walked away. Definitely too much attention.

"I'll get the EMT, make sure it's okay to leave."

Abby nodded, not raising her head. I waited a moment, not sure why, then left to get things settled.

At my text, Eli and Remi met us just down the street from the scene with an SUV. After throwing Abby's suitcase in the rear, I bundled her into the back seat, taking the spot beside her, Remi opposite me. Eli took off as soon as I had her secure.

Over Abby's head, I shot Remi an inquiring look.

"I was able to track them two streets over, to a van," Remi said, his voice quiet in the car. "Too many of them to take out on my own. They were alert."

They would be considering what they'd just done to draw attention to themselves. If I hadn't been focused on Abby, they'd all be dead.

"Same deal as the motorcycle: no plates, generic make and model. They were gone before I could grab transport to follow."

"Any feelers come back positive, Eli?" I asked.

Eli threw a glance over his shoulder, then turned back to watch the road. "Not yet. But that doesn't mean it won't. They're coming in hot and heavy. That won't go without notice."

I grunted in agreement.

Eli turned a corner, and Abby leaned hard against me. I couldn't stand it anymore. She might not want me to hold her, but I sure as fuck wanted to. I needed to hold her, to help her gather back together the pieces of herself that had shattered apart with the home she'd built.

So whether she wanted it or not, I put my arm around her. Her bones always felt fragile, delicate beneath my rough hands, as if the slightest touch might break her. It wouldn't—Abby gave as good as she got most times. The only time she broke was when she was beneath me, in climax.

She stiffened against my chest, tried to pull away. "Stop it," I hissed. "Just stop."

The words were low, though I had no doubt my brothers could hear them. I didn't care. All I cared about was touching her, holding her. Breathing in the smoky vanilla scent of her that reassured me she was alive.

I turned in the seat, gripped beneath her knees, and forced her legs over mine. Wrapped both arms around her, a shield from the rest of the world. Abby didn't protest again, but her barriers were up, her body tense. Holding a part of herself away. Protecting it. The only way I'd break through the barrier was with my body, my heat. Sex. But if I tried that tonight, I had a feeling she'd shatter, and not in a good way.

Let her resist me for now. I'd be waiting in the morning. This would all be waiting in the morning.

Chapter Six

I was lying on the bed when Abby came out of the shower. An ambush, she'd probably call it, though I'd say she ambushes me every time I see her like this. The towel around her body hid the details, but knowing what was beneath it with aching familiarity—it didn't matter how much she hid, I'd always want her.

But now wasn't the time for that. Now was the time to face reality.

She hadn't spoken to me since we'd arrived. The blank look in her eyes, like the entire day had been too much and she'd had to retreat for her own sanity, sliced through me like a KA-BAR every time I caught a glimpse of it. I needed to protect her—that thought went through my head on a continuous loop I couldn't seem to stop. I should be out there fixing this, hunting down the bastards who'd taken her home from her, erasing that guarded look from her eyes, but I couldn't. All I could do was rage inside and wait. I shouldn't be waiting while the woman I loved was in danger.

That's right. Love. I was in love with a woman who wanted to leave me behind.

Made perfect sense.

My breath hitched as an image of my parents the last time I saw them flashed in my mind. Dead. Covered in blood. That's what love led to.

And yet something inside me—a heart? A soul?—something deep refused to let go of the word as I watched Abby cross the room to her suitcase. I couldn't protect her from her attackers—yet—but I could keep her head out of the sand. It was the only way to save her right now.

"We need to talk."

I hated how everything that came out of my mouth sounded like I was barking orders. Some pansy-ass prince charming could probably soothe her, croon in her ear; I sounded like a drill sergeant whipping her into shape.

Abby ignored the demand and dug into her clothes. When she pulled out a pair of panties, a growl ripped from my chest.

"Save it, Levi."

I pushed to my feet. "Ignoring what happened won't make it go away. We have to deal—"

"What if I don't want to?" she snapped. Pajama bottoms came out next. "Maybe I just want to live in a fantasy world for one night. Reality is calling insurance companies and finding a new place to live. Reality is knowing someone hates me enough to bomb my house, and that you don't love me. Why would I want to face all that?"

She stood up, her pajamas gripped tight in one hand. Every line of her body rejected me, but I couldn't let it go. I couldn't let her go on believing...

"I never said I don't love you."

Abby scoffed. "You never said you do, either. You never said you want to build a life together. You never said you wanted a future."

Because a man like me doesn't have a future. "I'm an assassin," I pointed out. "I kill people for a living. What kind of future is that?"

Abby refused to look at me. "Exactly. No future." A sad grin pulled at her lips as she ran a hand through her wet hair. "Forgive me for finding that a little hard to face at the moment. I'll pick up my sword again tomorrow."

"Abby, I…"

But what could I say that would make it better. Hell, I couldn't even fault her for wanting to do nothing but forget for tonight. And she could do that better if I wasn't here—but fuck if I could make myself walk out that door.

Abby put a hand up, stopping me from saying anything more. "Forget it, Levi. I understand." She dropped her towel right where she stood, her creamy skin and rounded curves stopping my heart in its tracks. "I'm good enough to fuck, but not good enough to love. And don't deny it." She stepped into her pajama bottoms, her breasts swaying as she bent over. "If you loved me, we would be finding a way to make this work, not just finding a way for you to get me back into bed."

I stood, stunned, watching her pull her tank top over her head. I did love her; I knew that even if she didn't. Even if I had no practical idea of how it worked, what I felt couldn't be denied: This agony that exploded inside me every time I thought about her leaving, thought about *her*. The hunger that drilled through my marrow when I caught sight of her, saw her smile, forced her beneath me. The need to put her safety above my own—hell, above my own brothers. Damn it, of course it was love.

Which meant I was fucked no matter how this turned out. Damned if I do, damned if I don't.

So why deny myself?

My body went rigid as I stalked around the end of the bed. Abby's head came up fast, eyes wide, a doe about to be eaten. Sensing that she'd snapped some kind of leash that had held me in check so far. But no more. My body wanted what it wanted, and I would have it.

"Take those off," I said, nodding toward her clothes.

"No."

My expression told her exactly how long I'd allow that no to stand. Abby swallowed hard. Stepped back.

I kept right on coming.

"It's the only pair of pajamas you have, isn't it?"

Abby's leg banged against the corner of the bed. Her fists tightened in the fabric of her top. "Yes."

"Then I suggest you take them off."

She fumbled around the side of the bed. "Levi, I can't deal with this right now. With—"

"Me?" I chuckled, the sound low and angry. "I'm the bastard, right?" I moved closer. "Then this won't be a surprise, will it?"

I reached out; my fingers gripped the neck of her tee. One good tug and the fabric ripped down the center.

"Levi!"

There was anger in the word, yes, but also need. My woman needed to escape as much as I did—the pain, the uncertainty, the loss and fear. I could give her this.

I jerked the destroyed shirt down her arms. Her breasts bounced as she backed up again—right into the nightstand behind her.

I reached for her pajama bottoms.

Curbing the urge to rip, I took the pants all the way to the floor, then stared up at Abby from my position at her feet. Her breasts rose and fell with every hard gulp of air she took, her stomach quivering beneath her palms. I could see the heavy thud of her pulse in the side of her neck, the spot where she was both most vulnerable and most sensitive. I needed my mouth there, my teeth. I needed this too, to take her hard and fast and drown us both in the moment, crowding out everything else.

"This won't fix anything," she said.

At least she wasn't denying that it would happen. "It'll fix enough."

As I eased to my feet, her nipples went hard.

"This won't be slow," I warned her. But my fingers were, releasing the buttons on my shirt—one, two, three. Cool air hit my bare skin.

Abby's gaze zeroed in on my chest, the deep blue and red swirls of ink along my pecs, her eyes almost glowing, they were so fierce. "Does it matter?"

"No." All that mattered was taking her. Blanking her mind to anything but me.

Her breath shuddered as she drew it in. "Levi."

My gut clenched at the desire dripping from my name. "Little bird."

Goose bumps broke out across her skin. Her nipples tightened even more. When I went to work on the button of my jeans, she shifted restlessly.

"Get on the bed, little bird."

She hesitated as I slid my zipper down. My cock was hard enough to extend above the waistband of my boxer briefs, and the minute she saw it, her tongue skated across her bottom lip. My erection thumped against my belly. "Now, Abby."

Her eyes met mine, and the memories of the fire were gone. All that was on her mind was me. This. Us. When she turned to crawl onto the bed, triumph sparked in my veins.

Abby laid back, her ass on the edge, her wet hair spread across the sheets. Light played along the damp heat between her spread legs, making my mouth water.

"I want you on my tongue," I told her, toeing off my shoes. I let my jeans and underwear drop, my knees following, and then my mouth was on her pussy. Sharp, tangy cream flowed into me as I speared inside her, ruthlessly pursuing every drop of pleasure I could give her. I devoured her taste, her cries, her climb to the peak. When my thumb pressed hard against her clit, she exploded around my invasion.

I'd promised her fast, and that's what she was getting.

Her breath was still heavy as I shoved her up to the pillows. I didn't kiss her, didn't touch those beautiful breasts. No, I lined myself up and slammed inside her tight, wet heat, savoring the lingering spasms around my aching erection. Abby's keening wail split the air. Her knees came up, gripping my hips, tilting her pelvis so I could get in even deeper. Balls-deep. My cock head bumped her cervix and kicked in reaction.

I was home.

I planted my fists on either side of her body and brought my mouth to her then—nipping, licking, sucking. Stomach, ribs, the undersides of her breasts. She moaned and squirmed beneath me, trying to get me to move. And I did…when my lips surrounded one rock-hard nipple and I sucked her in. Her back bowed off the bed, arching up to me, sliding her pussy down my cock. I bit down on her nipple as I rammed back inside.

Abby clamped down hard around me.

Hurry. Hurry. Hurry. The words were a chant in my brain, my ears, and I followed their command to the letter. Every heavy, hasty thrust caught Abby's clit between our pelvic bones. Every suck and bite of her breast pushed her higher. Within a minute she was fisting my cock in another climax, nearly taking me over the edge with her.

Not yet. If the only thing I could give her was oblivion, then I'd do it right.

Only when she'd come twice more, her sweaty body collapsing beneath me, her eyes barely able to open, did I let myself go. One more thrust, two, and my cock spasmed hard in her wet depths, giving her everything I had to give.

When I could breathe again, I left the bed. Abby murmured a sleepy protest as I wiped her down with a cool washcloth, but otherwise she stayed asleep. After I'd cleaned myself up, I eased into the bed and pulled her onto my chest.

And there, in the darkness with Abby's scent surrounding me, her body warm and relaxed and satisfied against mine, I made myself a promise.

I was an assassin. I was ruthless. I wasn't going to give up the only woman who'd ever mattered to me, whether she wanted to walk away or not.

Chapter Seven

Abby was still sleeping when I slipped out of bed the next day. I'd lain beside her for a long time, watching her breathe, ready to slay dragons even if they appeared only in her sleep. When she didn't stir, I decided to conquer some real-world dragons instead.

Eli was busy at the computer, fingers flying as he stared down the screen like it was the enemy. Remi stood at the stove in the kitchen area, frying bacon. His bared chest left the scars from the gunshot that had almost killed him on full display, and like always, a well of nausea rose at the reminder. I'd almost lost my brother. I'd always believed we were damn near invincible until the day that sniper's shot had landed. Now I doubled down on never putting anyone in harm's way but me.

In the kitchen I retrieved a coffee cup and poured some. Black and almost strong enough to stand on its own—perfect. A few sips and I was ready to tackle business.

"What have we got, Eli?"

"Some interesting things." Eli spun his chair around and headed for the kitchen.

I gritted my teeth, wondering for the hundredth time how I could be related to someone so laid-back most of the time. "Like?"

Picking up a piece of bacon from the tray where Remi was depositing them as they finished, Eli held it thoughtfully in the air. "Like, we actually have even less on the van at Abby's than we got on the motorcycle in town. If we can't be close enough to follow, we aren't going to find these guys that way."

I cursed against the rim of my cup.

"We know they can't be local," Remi said, emphasizing the point with the tongs in his hand. "Word would've leaked somehow. So who do we know that's good enough to hide themselves that well when they aren't in their hometown?"

"I can think of a few US-based groups," I said. "The problem is narrowing it down to a specific group without being able to see their faces."

"Which I might have been able to do," Eli mumbled around a mouthful of bacon.

I snagged a couple of crispy strips off the tray as Remi switched from bacon to frying eggs. We all knew how to cook, but Remi was the best, hands down. "How?"

Eli moved to the fridge and began taking out juice and condiments. "Like you said, only certain groups are good enough to get away with this. My feelers in the southeastern US were getting me nowhere, so I started looking at other major cities where suspected groups were located. Turns out Rathlin's posse in DC has gone quiet over the last two days."

"They could be anywhere, including out of the country," Remi pointed out.

"True." The timer on the oven went off, and Eli pulled out a tray of biscuits. "I did look at more groups in the US, but they're the only one that appears to be a possibility. Plus…"

I grabbed a stack of plates from the cabinet. "Spit it out, dickhead. I'm tired of fishing."

Eli chuckled. "But stringing you along is so fun."

I glared his way, refusing to pass over the plates when he reached for them.

"Fine, fine. I did some analysis on the footage of the cyclist from yesterday. It seems likely that bike was driven by a woman."

I narrowed my eyes as Remi took the plates from my hands. "I don't know any major player with a woman on the team except—"

"Rathlin," we all said together.

Remi dished up the first batch of eggs, passing the plate to Eli. "Your reward."

Eli smirked and began loading bacon and biscuits on. Remi started another set of eggs.

"It could be someone new, someone we haven't heard of before," I pointed out.

"It could." Eli shrugged. "But DC makes sense if you think about it. With her father's connections, the idea that someone in the capital has it out for her isn't as far-fetched as, say, Douglas's group in SoCal."

Again, true. Still, my instincts weren't humming yet. I just wasn't sure why.

Remi passed over my eggs, and I joined Eli at the table. "I want you to get on the insurance stuff today, Remi. As much as we can get taken care of without Abby worrying, I want done."

"Don't you think you should talk to me about that first?" a husky feminine voice asked behind me.

My grip on my fork tightened. "No, little bird, I don't." Putting my fork down, I turned in my seat. Abby walked through the open living area, her body concealed by her pajama pants and an oversize sweatshirt. Her arms were crossed as if holding herself together with the tight grip, and dark circles painted the skin under her eyes. The sight of her made me ache in more ways than one.

"Get some sleep?" I asked, knowing I shouldn't. Knowing I was just pissing her off.

"You know I did."

Her tone said *as if I had a choice.* I couldn't keep the self-satisfied grin off my face.

Abby dropped her eyes and moved to the coffeepot. After pouring what was left into an empty cup, she began a new pot. She'd spent enough time with us to know any coffee we made required a steel gut to consume. As she waited for it to brew, she moved to a nearby plug and hooked up her phone to charge, studiously ignoring my stare.

Remi passed over a plate after she'd filled her own cup. "Sit and eat, Abby. You'll need it today."

I noticed she didn't argue with him, though she didn't sit with us—she stood at the bar, where she sipped and ate and scrolled through her phone. When she began typing out a message, my eyes narrowed.

"Who are you texting?"

"Charlotte."

I glanced at my brothers, both of whom shrugged. "Charlotte who?"

Abby didn't look up from her phone. "You'd know if you bothered to stick around during the day."

I half rose from my seat, determined to grab her cell and shut it down, hide her from the world. A sharp shake of Remi's head had me easing back into my chair.

We ate in loaded silence for a few minutes. Not long after Remi joined us, the other cell phone on the countertop vibrated, the one I'd given as a contact point last night. I stood to answer.

"Agozi here."

"Mr. Agozi, this is Detective Roger Bryant." The man's gravelly voice grated on my nerves. "How are you and Ms. Roslyn this morning?"

Low on sleep and good will if Abby's glance meant anything. "We're fine, thank you. What can I do for you, Bryant?"

The entire room perked up, all eyes locked on me.

"I'd like you both to come down to the station today if possible."

And by *I'd like*, I was sure he meant *I demand.* "For…?"

"Just a second interview," Bryant said. "See if we can help you remember anything more."

No fucking way that was all the man wanted. "When?"

"Noon."

It wasn't a question, of course. "We'll be there."

Satisfaction colored Bryant's, "Thank you."

I ended the call and looked up at three pairs of questioning eyes. "That man is going to be a problem."

"The detective from last night?" Abby asked.

I grunted a reply.

"He's just a cop," Eli pointed out.

"No, he's not." I returned to my seat at the table, my arm brushing Abby's as I passed. "He was part of the team that investigated our parents' murders."

Curses erupted from both Remi and Eli.

"What does he want?" Abby asked.

"Us, there. For more questioning." I glanced at the clock on the microwave. "Can you be ready in an hour?"

Abby crammed the last bite of biscuit into her mouth while shooting me a mean look. A moment later she was heading for the bedroom.

Exactly where I needed her to be.

"E—"

His hand came up before I could even get his full name out. "Dig up everything I can on the douchebag cop, his partner, his family, his cat... I know, I know." He grabbed his plate and Abby's and headed for the sink.

"You want me with you at the station?" Remi asked.

I thought about that one a minute. Having two guards for Abby would be best, but... "No. The less exposure we have, the better. He's already talked to me."

Remi glanced at the bedroom, then met my gaze again, one eyebrow raised. "I wasn't worried about Bryant. I'm more worried about a buffer between you and her."

I gave him my best keep-it-up-and-you're-dead smile. "Piss off."

Remi shrugged, but I caught his grin as he took his plate over to the sink. My hand hit the back of his head as he passed. "Shut up."

He snorted. "Make me, dickhead."

Impossible. If I'd learned anything in the nineteen years since we'd been on our own, that was it. Running mouths and rampant opinions were a given. Unless we were on an op—then everyone deferred to me.

Everyone except Abby.

Chapter Eight

A police station was not the ideal place for a man like me, but that wasn't why I tensed as we walked up the front steps. No, it was the visceral assault of memories that had me wanting to escape so hard I was sweating.

Abby brushed her hand along my bicep, seeming to sense my anxiety. She always did, even though I'd long ago perfected hiding my emotions. Hopefully no one here had her ability to see through my disguises.

A single touch wasn't enough. As she passed through the door I held open for her, I settled my palm at the small of her back. Guiding her, yes, but also reminding myself. This is who I was now, the man whose simple touch could connect me with the most important person in my world.

Not the eleven-year-old boy who'd been filled with so much fear and grief and rage that he'd thrown up every time his uncle brought him here.

Even the smell was the same. Garbage, coffee, and chemical air freshener that couldn't mask the underlying age and decay of the building and its inhabitants. We crossed the foyer to the front desk, the ring of my boots on the bleached tiles an echo of my past, a death knell that urged me over and over to flee. Back then, it was Amos Agozi's cruel hand digging into my thin, bony shoulder that kept me moving forward. Now it was the discipline I'd built over a lifetime of survival, of killing. I knew what had to be done to get what we needed: information. I'd face my demons for Abby; nobody else.

"May I help you?" the man behind the desk asked.

"We have an appointment with Detective Bryant," Abby said. I watched the man soften as he eyed her, the glimmer of attraction sparking in his expression. A little younger than me, without the hard edge I'd cultivated all my life. Did Abby want someone like him? Would her life be easier if I left her to find a man without my baggage?

Easier, maybe, but not safer. She might deserve a man like him, but she wasn't going to get one.

"Of course," he said, his gaze sliding to me as he reached for his phone. Not quite meeting my eyes. He knew a predator when he saw one.

We waited a few minutes before Bryant came to collect us. Following him to his office was a walk through the Twilight Zone—a sense of unreality, like this just couldn't be happening. I hadn't felt that way as a child, too scared of what Amos would do to me. To my brothers. I'd walked in on the man with his gun raised, pointed at my dead parents on their bloody bed. When he'd swung that gun toward me, I'd thought I would die. Almost wanted to.

But Remi and Eli had needed me. And Amos had needed a witness to corroborate his story—an intruder in the million-dollar mansion, motive unknown.

Even as a child I'd known Amos would only need us for so long. Then we'd be as dead as my parents.

"I tell ya," Bryant said as he escorted us into his office, "I can't get over the déjà vu here."

No joke.

I gave Bryant what he was expecting, clearing my throat of the gravel that had built up on the long walk through the halls. "Yeah, this is not something I ever expected to relive."

"I imagine not." The man's gaze was hardened by years of seeing the worst in life, much like mine was, but not without a touch of sympathy. "I've never forgotten your parents' case; I hope you know that. Never regretted not finding a perp more."

I nodded abruptly. "You said you needed to follow up on some things from last night?"

Bryant eyed me a half minute more before turning his attention to the open file on his desk. "Of course." He folded his hands on the scarred wooden surface, leaning forward. "You said you arrived at the house shortly before the incident, is that correct?"

I relaxed into my chair, letting the focus fall to Abby.

"We did. Maybe ten minutes before?" She glanced at me. I nodded.

"And you parked in the garage." Bryant looked at the papers under his hands.

"Yes. My car was already there, but we pulled Levi's SUV in as well."

I was still pissed over losing the vehicle. Not that I couldn't replace it; I could, five times over, without blinking an eye. Death paid big-time. It was the principle of it—any loss came far too close to Abby.

Who continued to answer questions, even as she shifted in her seat, crossing her legs. Bryant might've thought she was uncomfortable with him, but I knew better. Her feet didn't touch the floor; she was uncomfortable in the chair. My little bird.

I couldn't believe I actually knew enough about a woman to realize that she was too short for a seat. Or to care that she was uncomfortable, but my first instinct was to find her somewhere else to sit. The blend of surprise and satisfaction that accompanied the knowledge was far more pleasurable than the sweat-inducing memories that had filled my head minutes ago.

"Anyone watching the house would've seen you arrive," Bryant said thoughtfully.

"Of course." Abby's tone said she was confused about the detective's focus. So was I.

"What are you thinking, Bryant?" I asked gruffly.

He picked up a slender silver pen from his desk and tapped the end on the papers.

Tap. Tap. Tap.

"I'm thinking, why would someone attack, knowing a big, scary guy like you was around? Why not wait till Ms. Roslyn was alone, unprotected?"

Damn it, he was right. My presence should've been a deterrent. Mine and Remi's? No one should've come within a hundred yards of the place. And I knew they would've seen us both through the windows.

It made no sense.

Abby was looking between the two of us, still confused. Without thinking I reached for her hand, hating the way it trembled in mine.

"I know you were young when your parents died," Bryant said, "but I'm assuming since your uncle's death that you're aware of the contents of your father's will."

What did that have to do with anything? "My uncle was a bastard, Bryant. He shipped us off to boarding school the second he could." Or at least that's the story he used, as I found out later. "When I was finally able to, I made sure my brothers and I were as far away from him as we could possibly get. And never looked back."

"Shame." Bryant tapped some more. "Your uncle was also murdered. Also unsolved. Unusual in the same family. But I did some digging." He shuffled aside some of the papers until he found what he was looking for. "It appears your father's will stated that everything be held in trust for his children. If his wife also died, his brother was to be the executor of the will."

"Right." My father hadn't known his brother would betray him.

"But…Amos Agozi died before the three of you, so your father's lawyer took Amos's place as executor."

I hadn't gone looking for a fortune when I killed Amos eleven years ago, only revenge. My brothers and I didn't need the money, so I hadn't even considered finding out what happened to it.

Bryant passed over the paper in his hand. "Oddly enough, the trust your father set up reverts to your full control when you turn thirty."

"What?"

I scanned the document, the legalese skimming off my brain. All I could focus on was that word, *thirty*, near the bottom. My next birthday. And it was coming up, less than a month from now.

Thirty.

The implications buzzed in my head like a thousand angry bees. "Fuck."

"Exactly."

The puzzle pieces fell into place, a grim picture that made my stomach roll. "You think this wasn't about Abby."

Abby tensed beside me. Guilt began a slow crawl over my body.

"Unfortunately," Bryant was saying, "I think last night has very little to do with Ms. Roslyn other than proximity."

Proximity. Bile rose in the back of my throat.

"Though it's too early to be certain, I can find no credible threat to her. Nothing has churned up on her father's case, no concerning discoveries or enemies coming to light."

"But if whoever this was saw us arrive, knew I was there…" And Remi. Kill two birds with one stone.

And then there was the attack on the street, the one Bryant didn't know about. Remi had been with Abby then. With a ball cap over his dark blond hair, he could easily have been mistaken for me.

The meeting hadn't been a setup for Abby. It had been a setup *for me*. But how had they linked us together?

I took a deep, shaky breath, desperate to keep the contents of my stomach where they were. *Abby lost her house because of me.* I couldn't look at her, couldn't stand to face the devastation, the accusation that might be in her eyes.

"I've only been able to make cursory inquiries so far." Bryant picked his pen back up. "But one thing did give me pause. Do you know who your father's lawyer was?"

I'd been eleven years old the last time I heard that information; I hadn't cared. "No."

"Alan Chadwick. Of Manassas, Chadwick, and Heinz."

I jolted in my seat.

"Heinz?" Abby asked. "Lance Heinz?"

"Yeah." Bryant tilted his head. "You know him?"

I squeezed Abby's hand, willing her not to say anything more. Bryant would find out soon enough, maybe, but we needed time to put more pieces together, do our own investigation before evidence started disappearing into police custody.

"My father was a politician," she said, her tone even. "I know—and have entertained—just about every lawyer in town."

"Well you won't be entertaining Heinz anymore," Bryant said. "He's dead."

Abby's surprise looked believable even to me. My woman had spent years acting happy under her father's thumb; she knew how to project just the right emotion. But I could read beneath her mask just as well as she could mine, see the pain lurking there. She was hurting.

I needed to get her out of here. *I* needed to get out of here.

"So what's your theory, Detective?"

Bryant spread his hands wide. "Right now I'm leaving all avenues open. But I will be meeting with Mr. Chadwick. And doing more digging. In the meantime I think it's important that you both proceed with caution."

I nodded. "Abby has an excellent security team at her disposal. We've already called them in." Not that we'd ever been out.

"I'd also like to meet with your brothers, see if they remember anything that might help us."

"Are you reopening my parents' case?"

"Not formally." Bryant narrowed his eyes, the bulldog expression making me wary. "But I can't deny that there might be a connection."

"My brothers no longer live in town," I lied. "I'll check with them and see what they might know."

Bryant didn't like the evasion; I could tell. "Or you could give me their numbers. I could call."

I stood. "Let me talk to them first. As you can understand, this is a sensitive subject. I'll have them contact you soon."

He didn't argue further, but as we said our goodbyes, Bryant's focus on me never relented. The man wasn't about to give up, not now. I'd been right all along. Good cop or not, he was definitely going to be a problem.

Chapter Nine

There was a period in my life when being alone wasn't possible. With two kids to protect and take care of, my time wasn't my own. When my brothers were old enough, I would sometimes go out for a ride on the old Harley I'd managed to rebuild from junkyard parts, or sit for a couple of hours beneath the stinging pain of a tattoo needle, letting it wash away the nightmares. Neither was an option today.

But I had to get away.

The ride back to the warehouse had been silent. Not because we were lost in our thoughts. I simply couldn't bring myself to open my mouth. I mean, what the hell was I going to say? *Your life is totally fucked up because of me. You probably hate me—and who could blame you—but I couldn't have known.*

Maybe that wasn't totally true. Maybe, if I hadn't been hiding from my past, so fiercely focused on the now, this could have been avoided.

I'd shared sex and laughter and agony with the woman beside me, but I realized now that all the emotion had been on her side. I loved her, I knew that, but I hadn't truly shared that with her. Hunger, yes, but not love, not till I'd been confronted with her leaving. The laughter had come from her, the agony too. I knew in my gut that she wanted me to give those things back to her, to share it all, carry each other's burdens, but this...it was too intimate. A weapon that could shatter me. A box that could very well explode in my face.

Or it might have already. Because just as I hadn't spoken, neither had Abby.

I pulled up to the door of the warehouse, but instead of turning the SUV off, I let it idle. Abby didn't miss that fact.

"You're not coming in."

If I'd wanted to keep everything in my life just as it was, I shouldn't have fixated on such a smart woman. "I need a little time."

She faced me in her seat. I waited in the silence, knowing she wanted me to look at her, but the shame that had engulfed me at the station felt like a mold around my body, paralyzing me. Freezing me from the inside out.

Her palm settled on my jaw, the warmth of her sizzling through my frostbitten skin. I gasped at the heat.

"Levi."

"What?"

There were so many things she could say, some of them cruel, all of them true. She didn't say any of them. Not aloud. Instead she nudged my head up just enough that her mouth could settle against mine.

It wasn't a passionate kiss. The casual observer would've labeled it platonic, maybe sweet. It wasn't about sex. That simple touch—Abby's lips and mine—was an affirmation. I opened my eyes and stared into hers and saw…everything. And nothing. No judgment, no blame. Just all the love that she somehow contained in her delicate body, enough to cover and comfort and connect us both. She could manage that all on her own, with more emotion in her little finger than I'd probably allowed myself to feel in a lifetime.

But I didn't want her to do it alone. I wanted it all, everything, with her.

So I opened my mouth. Took over. Delved into the sweetness that was Abby, greed roaring to life inside me at the flavor of her on my tongue. And when she moaned in pleasure? All I wanted was to get down on my knees and beg her to stay with me. To never leave, not even for a second.

Except that's what I was planning to do right now, wasn't it?

I drew back, easing her down with little licks and sucks and brushes of skin on skin. She seemed as reluctant to open her eyes as I was to end the kiss, but I had no choice.

"Look at me, little bird."

She did. Worry and wonder swirled in her gaze, and I felt my heart break a little bit more. I'd borne the pain of solitude most of my life; how had I managed to gain something so precious?

"I won't be long; I promise. Eli and Remi…" I cleared my throat. "I need to tell them, but I need my head on straight first."

The door to the warehouse opened in my peripheral vision, and Eli stepped out. Abby glanced at him, then back to me. Her finger traced my cheek, my lips.

"I don't blame you, Levi. You know that, right?"

A flush went through me. "You should."

"No, I shouldn't, any more than I should blame your brothers." She tapped lightly on my bottom lip. "You'll see it my way once you have time to consider it."

That was never gonna happen. "I will?"

"Of course you will." A spark of mischief lit in her eyes.

"Why?"

"Because I said so, and I'm always right."

Unbelievably, a grin curved the corner of my lips. "You're getting a bit big for your britches."

"Hmm." Abby reached for the door handle. "If that keeps up, you might have to take them off and spank me."

How could she do this to me, put things into perspective when all I wanted to do was wallow in their heaviness? "I don't need an excuse to spank you; you know that."

One last look from those mysterious hazel eyes before she gripped the door. "I do. Now hurry back so you can follow through."

A bark of laughter escaped me before the door slammed shut. Abby didn't look back as she walked toward Eli. He let her in, giving me a finger wave, then allowed the door to close behind him. I put the SUV in gear again and headed for the highway.

Outside the city, rolling Georgia hills and winding country roads predominated. Almost idyllic. As a child I'd known this country so well, but it's hard to steal when homes and businesses are few and far between. Especially stealing enough to support three growing boys. The city had been our only option, but I'd never forgotten what it felt like to be back home.

Well, not home anymore. I didn't know who the mansion my parents had raised us in belonged to. Probably sold somewhere along the way, to another millionaire, single or married, maybe filling the house with kids. Knowing it, seeing it would've shattered the memories inside me—of two parents, three boys, together. Safe.

My uncle might've killed them for their money, but he couldn't kill the memories. Someone taking our place could.

And yet now, with the residue of the police station tainting me, I couldn't stop myself from driving toward the back of the wooded estate where we'd lived. A two-lane road bordered the creek curving along the boundary of the property. Rocks jutting up forced the water to twirl and dance, to sing a song as it tumbled over them. I'd heard its music in my dreams for years after we left, and yet as I parked the SUV amid some overgrown bushes and walked to the edge of the water, that familiarity was distant, hidden behind a veil of something I wasn't sure I could name.

That veil protected me as I found a shallow area to cross, then the rock-studded path my brothers and I used to follow down to the water. The woods enveloped me like warm arms, pulling me back to a childhood most would call idyllic. Wholesome. Years spent roaming the land, playing sports, milk and cookies after school. And my mother…God, my mother.

She'd been so soft—her voice, her smile. But not her hugs; those had been fierce, tight. The memory of those hugs almost ripped through the veil. The crackle of a walkie-talkie up ahead was the only thing that saved me.

Son of a bitch.

I stepped into the underbrush, cursing myself for being that careless. Crouching behind the thick trunk of an old maple, I waited, watching, listening.

Moments later a black-clad, muscular guard passed along the trail, radio to his mouth. Reporting the all clear. He was almost as much of a fool as I'd been.

When he passed, I turned to head back to the car. No need to follow up my first visit to the cops in years with a second for trespassing. But my first glimpse of the man's back brought me up short. A scope site outlined in white, the words *Rathlin Security* marching across it.

Everything in me went still.

The guard moved on, oblivious to the threat mere feet away. Comfortable on his own turf; too comfortable. He'd make that mistake in the future and pay for it. Today I had better things to do than teach him the lesson he needed to learn.

I made for the house.

My father had been smart. As much as he'd loved the Georgia countryside, no man with that much money was without enemies, and he'd made security a priority. Several acres surrounding the house had been totally cleared, leaving nowhere for the enemy to hide. That worked against me, but familiarity was my ally. Circling the edge of the woods, I came to the area where Remi and I had spent our final summer here. In an ancient oak thick with foliage, we'd spent hours carrying old boards and limbs to build the beginnings of our very own fort. More of a platform, really. Even the ragged rope my father had given us to climb into the tree still dangled, more frayed than ever, waiting for the boys who'd never come back.

The man, though…

I avoided the rope—no way would it take my weight now. But a quick scramble up the twisted branches of the tree got me to the platform. Ignoring the twinges of painful memories in the back of my mind, my heart, I eased onto the old boards and laid out flat.

Still the perfect vantage point to see the house.

A small set of foldable binoculars in my fatigues pocket came in handy. I lay, listening to the creak and strain of the wood, and watched as what looked like a small army went in and out of the three-story, sprawling stone mansion that used to be my home.

Many of the upper windows—the living areas— were blocked by curtains. My parents had used the lower floor primarily for entertaining, and it looked as if the setup was similar now, as many of those windows were clear enough to see the men lingering in the rooms. They certainly weren't hiding their presence, nor did they appear to be worried about an attack. Though there were plenty of weapons on display, they were all holstered or waiting at fingertips, not at the ready.

These men weren't worried. But if they were who I thought they were, they should be.

A flurry of activity accompanied the arrival of a sleek black limo at the door. The driver exited the vehicle, going around to await his passengers. A second vehicle, this one a solid black SUV—the kind I preferred—pulled up behind.

The door to the mansion opened.

A contingent of six men, all armed, all with semiautomatics in hand, came out. They lined the sidewalk, at the ready.

A pause.

A new figure exited, this one familiar. I knew that swarthy skin, broken nose, and thick hair and beard. Rathlin.

I saved my curses for later and waited, eyes trained on the scene.

Two men stepped from the house and stopped at the top of the stairs. Both in suits. I could make out the features of the one facing me as they talked—salt-and-pepper hair, glasses. Classic metro. Was this the lawyer, Chadwick?

Had to be. But the man with him, built like a bull and big enough to block Chadwick completely from sight when he shifted to the side…I didn't recognize him. Maybe if I could see his face.

But he never turned. With a few words to Chadwick, punctuated with a thick finger stabbed in the lawyer's direction, the man returned to the house, never giving me his front. I tucked the scene away for further analysis later. For now, I had somewhere else to be.

I made it to the river without incident, and found my car undisturbed. Further evidence that the earlier guard needed to be canned. I waited till the convoy carrying Chadwick passed behind me, pulled out carefully, and followed.

Chapter Ten

The limo peeled off when we arrived at the loop around the outskirts of the city. Chadwick going home or to his office, no doubt. I was more interested in where the mercenaries were headed. When they took the exit that would get them to the warehouse, I called Remi.

"Get Abby out of there."

A heavy sigh came through the line. "Why?"

"Because a six-pack of Rathlin's men are headed your way. Maybe they followed us after the fire, maybe they're just scoping out the area, I don't know, but I won't take chances with her."

Remi swore. The sound of his boots on the concrete echoed in my ear. "She's not gonna be happy about this. Again."

"You're not letting my woman get to you, are you?"

"I'm letting your drama get to me." I could hear irritation in his voice, but underneath, something else, something deadly serious. "Is this all really worth it? She's not a toy you can keep, brother."

For a moment the road before me sheeted red. "Shut the fuck up and get her out of there."

Remi grunted a reply and hung up on me. That was okay. He'd do as I said whether he agreed with me or not.

And that was a good thing, because the SUV stopped a half-dozen blocks from the location of the warehouse and disgorged three of its passengers. They spread out, obviously canvassing the area. Shit.

I got Eli on the line as I followed the vehicle down the road.

"Yeah."

"Heads-up, E. We've got a crew in the area."

I could hear the tap of his fingertips on the keys. He hummed in my ear for a moment. "You're awfully close to 'em," he finally said.

I narrowed my eyes on the SUV as it turned left near St. Michael's, the only building in the area with a structure tall enough for surveillance—the steeple. We were definitely being scoped out. "They're headed for the church. Please tell me Remi has Abby out of there."

As if he would dare not obey. Eli chuckled. "She went nicely with her jailer, yes. Had a few choice words for you, though."

When was she going to understand that this was all to keep her safe?

"She does get it," Eli said, startling me. It was only then that I realized I'd asked the question aloud. "She's afraid, and unlike us, she can't shoot right into action to fix the problem. Railing against the injustice of it is the only outlet she has for her frustration."

God, I hoped he was right. And said so as I pulled into a parking space two streets down from the church.

"When am I ever not right?"

If we'd been in the same room, I would've flipped him the bird. "Keep it up, little bro. I'm keeping track."

"Hey, I'm no kid in need of discipline anymore. We're not keeping score."

He sounded a bit too defensive to be sure. I grinned. "You're not."

But I wasn't either, not really. I was distracting myself. Remi would keep Abby safe, I knew, but I wanted to be the one with her. And yes, as always, what I wanted and what was necessary almost never coincided.

I stepped out of the SUV, the calm of battle settling on my shoulders. "Visual."

Eli rattled off the group's position, then the individuals. "Definitely doing a sweep. Which way you going?"

I eyed the steeple at St. Michael's. "I'll keep a watch here. Just don't let 'em sneak up on me."

The first head appeared in the small window at the steeple. They'd be setting up surveillance equipment now. "Any sign they're focused on the warehouse?"

"Nah." Wheels rattled as Eli rolled his chair around. "Either they don't know for certain we're here, or they're just getting the lay of the land."

Too bad for them we wouldn't be here after tonight. The location was compromised; all that was left was to squeeze our opponents for whatever details we could get before we ghosted.

"Thoughts on which of those three unknowns would sing the loudest?" I asked, knowing Eli would get my drift.

A weighted silence fell as he considered his answer. Then a laugh. "I'm going to go with the one that just took a whiz on the back corner of our location without realizing where he actually was."

"Sounds clueless," I said. "What intel could he possibly give us?"

"Doesn't matter. His bladder is empty; that means I won't be cleaning up piss at the end of the night."

And the youngest always got the cleanup. "You're in luck. We won't be back, so no need for cleanup."

"Then let's go for a smart one."

After a bit of debate we decided on the guy that we only caught glimpses of—harder to catch but more likely to have what we needed. But harder to catch. I figured being up front was our best bet.

Joining Eli in the warehouse, I proceeded to wait till our man came sniffing around. Alone. When he got close enough, I opened the door.

"Looking for me?"

"Motherfuck—"

He was too focused on me to notice Eli behind him, at least not until the needle penetrated his ass. His elbow connected with my brother's nose—Eli was too busy pressing the plunger to see it coming—and then the mercenary hit his knees. I caught him before he did a face-plant on the concrete.

Eli had tears and blood streaming down his face. "You're supposed to duck," I reminded him.

"Shuh de fuh up."

We grabbed both sides of the man's collar and dragged him into the warehouse.

"Yoo—" Eli stopped, shook his head. He dropped his handful and made a gesture that could either mean *go fuck yourself, asshole* or *tie him up yourself.* Maybe both. I bet on the latter and pulled the deadweight over to the chair already set up for our guest. By the time he stirred, he was trussed tighter than a Thanksgiving turkey.

"What the…fu…wha—" He shook his head groggily. I let him soak for a few more minutes, giving the last of the sedative time to dissipate.

Eli wandered up with a bag of frozen peas plastered to his face. The look he gave the man in the chair could've felled the enemy at fifty feet, much less five.

The man was awake enough to grin.

Eli huffed.

Worked for me. "He's all yours, E."

I gave my brother twenty minutes. Plenty of time to rough the guy up a little, for which I did not feel guilty. Rathlin's group wasn't known for caring about the innocent, and from the insignia on this guy's jacket, he'd been involved with Rathlin for quite a while.

When I figured he was loose enough, I signaled Eli to back off.

"Look," I said, coming to stand square in front of him. "I'm not interested in killing you. I also don't want this to take all day. Just tell me what the fuck y'all are after so I can kick your ass out the door."

The guy turned his head and spit. "Fuck off."

"I take it that means you won't cooperate."

He stared up at me, defiance in his eyes, lips tight. I shrugged. "Bring me the Taser," I told Eli.

The guy scoffed. "Really?"

"Oh, this?" Eli held up the small black rectangle. "We made a few modifications. No darts; that's nice. More direct current—not so nice. Have you had an enema today? No? You might wish you had in a few minutes."

Eli handed me the Taser. I flipped the switch and touched the pointed end to the man's chest. He grunted quietly, then laughed.

"He doesn't think we'll do anything," Eli said. His voice took on an evil glee. "Stick him again."

I tipped my head toward my brother. "We need to give him at least one more chance. You know how I feel about this."

Eli rolled his eyes. "Every torture victim is someone's son or daughter," he said in a singsong voice. "I know."

I really did feel that way. Not that this guy was going to care. I raised my eyebrow. "Last chance, asshole—what do y'all want?"

"I already gave you my answer: fuck you."

I turned the dial on the Taser a couple of clicks. What happened next wasn't pretty. When he finally quit twitching, I asked again, "What does Chadwick want? Is this about the trust? Because I don't give a shit about the money."

The man worked his mouth for a minute, finally shook his head.

Okay.

This time was worse. The guy threw up after; for a minute I thought his stomach would actually come up, he clenched so hard. I stood impassively, waiting for the retching to stop. "Tell me what I want to know. What does Chadwick want?"

The man gave a watery growl. "Chadwick is a pissant."

"Meaning what?" Eli asked.

No answer. Another zap.

"Here's what I don't get it," I said while his teeth rattled in the aftermath. "Why kill me over a trust?

The man has to have more money than he knows what to do with, especially after eleven years of skimming. Or is he just trying to avoid someone finding out the trust is empty?" Not the most likely possibility, but who knew?

A weak grin pulled at the man's mouth. "You think this is about money?" A sick laugh left him. "Have you even read that trust?"

I frowned.

Eli had wandered over to the computer station. "Bro."

I walked toward him, giving our guest time to breathe. "Yeah?"

"We got a couple of hounds."

Sure enough, someone was sniffing around outside. Guess they'd found Eli's blood on the pavement. "It's your lucky day, dude." I stuck the Taser in my pocket. "We'll let your friends clean up." I walked over and leaned down, eye to eye. "Take my advice—find out a bit about your target before you go after them."

"We know all about you, fucker."

I glanced at his bonds. "Obviously not enough." I narrowed my eyes. "And if you think I won't come after you, your boss, and the rest of his toy-soldier army, you're fucking delusional. This is child's play. Quit while you're ahead."

Chapter Eleven

"About damn time."

Remi's words were thrown at me as I stepped through the door of the two-bedroom bungalow where he'd taken Abby. Unfortunately they weren't as welcoming as the mellow colors of the living room, which, after the day that I'd had, only served to piss me off.

"You got a problem with me doing my job, brother?"

"What I've got is places to be."

What the fuck? I eyed his closed-off expression as he jerked on his jacket. The attitude wasn't new, though Remi never showed it around Abby. Since he'd healed from the gunshot wound, he'd had spells where his usually grounded outlook was submerged beneath an anger I didn't quite understand. And disappearances that made me uneasy. "Like where?"

"Out."

I grabbed his arms as he brushed past me. "Where's Abby?"

Remi kept his gaze on the door, his body vibrating with the need to escape. "Taking a bath."

The words sent a rush of blood to my lower belly, but I ignored it. "You know we're gonna have to talk about this, right?"

"About what?" Remi met my eyes finally, his own so dark I couldn't read them. "About how much time I spend watching your woman while you're off playing the fucking hero?"

I narrowed my eyes at him but didn't rise to the bait, mostly because I didn't want Abby to hear him talking like that. She wasn't a burden, and I wouldn't have anyone telling her she was. And I knew Remi didn't mean it that way. He had a chip on his shoulder directed at me and me alone; I just couldn't figure out where it was coming from.

And tonight I didn't give a shit. I released his arm. "Check in with one of us in the morning."

He needed time? I'd give it. An entire night off. After the session with Rathlin's man earlier, I didn't think we had anything to worry about. Not till we dug up some answers.

Remi smirked, but a single arched brow was enough warning for him to zip his lips. He was out the door before I could say another word.

I locked up behind him and set the security system to on. Weariness hit me as I crossed the room. It shouldn't; physically today had been nothing special. And yet I felt like I'd been hit by a damn two-by-four. Every muscle in my body ached. All I wanted was to forget, and my feet took me across the room instinctively, down the hall, into the master bedroom until I faced the closed bathroom door that separated me from the sweetest oblivion I'd ever tasted. I might never deserve it, but I sure as hell craved it.

I reached for the doorknob, turned it.

Abby lay back in the garden tub along the far wall, her hair in a knot at the top of her head, eyes closed. Candlelight flickered across her creamy skin, and I wondered for a moment where Remi had found the candles. Say what he might, he definitely had a soft spot for my woman. We all did.

Especially me. An assassin with a weakness I couldn't deny. I stood in the doorway and soaked in the sight of her, letting her seep into my pores all over again.

"Stop staring, you pervert."

A grin flashed over my lips as I straightened. Abby's ability to make me smile shouldn't surprise me, but it did, every damn time. "Staring at a beautiful woman doesn't make me a pervert."

Moving inside, I closed the door behind me.

"It does if she's naked."

"You like for me to look at you naked."

"I do." Her smile was soft, almost lazy as she stretched in the water. Obviously the warmth had managed to ease her tension by now.

I wanted nothing more than to climb into that tub with her and do things that really would be perverted in her eyes, but I couldn't, not yet. Not with the stench of the job, of violence coating every inch of me. So I moved to the shower instead. Abby's knowing gaze followed me as I turned the water on, then stripped my clothes, dropping them in a heap in the corner.

There was something disturbingly domestic about sharing a bathroom. As if I was somehow normal, just a man living with his woman, a regular nine-to-five job, maybe a dog or a kid. None of that would ever be me, but Abby made the dream come alive sometimes. One of the reasons I'd kept myself away from her for so damn long. We both knew how that had turned out. But unlike Abby, I understood, deep down to the core of who I was, that normal would never be an option for me.

I left the shower without drying off. Abby sat up in the tub and turned the spigot on, adding hot water to her cooling bath. I didn't care if it was frigid; I couldn't resist her lure a moment longer. My dick was already hard, my heart speeding up, mouth watering. The need went far beyond anything I could ever put into words. I needed her too much for her own good, but I couldn't stay the fuck away, no matter how much I should.

Her gaze trailed along my body like a touch— shoulders, chest, hips, cock. I was already stretched to my limit, but that didn't stop me from swelling even more, as if my erection needed to prove how much it wanted her. The animal inside me raised its head. It had been denied the kill earlier, but here the prey was much tastier.

I stepped into the water. Abby turned the spigot off with one hand and rested the other on my calf, sliding upward. My groan had very little to do with the hot water encasing my body as I lowered into it, and everything to do with the tightening of my balls as her hand crept higher.

There were things we needed to discuss, decisions to be made—and argued over, if I knew Abby, and I did—but not here, not now. When her palm slipped around to cup my ass, my restraint broke.

Resting back against the slope of the tub, I jerked her over my body. The wet heat of her core, so much hotter than the water surrounding us, slid along my cock, nearly crossing my eyes with the pleasure. When her opening met my tip, I had to drive inside. There was no controlling it. No way that savage part of me could wait.

She wasn't quite ready; her sudden gasp, the balling of her fists on my pecs told me that. But she didn't protest. I felt her go tight, fighting the invasion; then, with a heavy exhale, she softened and let me in.

And goddamn, it was good. Abby above me, enveloping me. Heat and steam and vanilla flowers filled my senses as I stared into her hazel eyes. This was as close to heaven as my blackened soul would ever be allowed to get.

Until she leaned in, her breasts pillowing against my hard chest, her plump lips settling against mine, and proved me wrong.

I opened beneath her. Let her all the way in. Her invasion drew a knot deep in my pelvis, curling my hips, my cock desperate to move, but I refused to give in, to rush any more than I already had. Instead I sucked lightly at her tongue, felt her pelvis tilt to grind her clit against me, and growled at the pleasure that speared through my veins.

Abby was the one who broke the kiss. She sat up, letting me sink even deeper inside. I threw my head back, gripping her hips to hold her still. "Abby…"

Her name came out strangled. She clamped down on my cock.

"Little bird, stop."

Abby peeled my hands from her hips and moved them to her breasts. Her hard nipples scraped my palms. "Can't," she said tightly.

"Shit."

Gripping her ribs, I drew her closer until her breasts were all I could see, opened my mouth around one strawberry-pink nipple, and sucked it in.

Abby's cries echoed in my ears as I devoured her. That's what she was, a feast. Lush and tasty. I wanted to gorge on every inch of her. She writhed in my arms, but my hold kept her from doing more than squirming on the end of my cock, the constant pressure threatening to blow off the top of my head. I sucked harder, desperate to drive her as wild as I was, to get as much of her inside me as I could, but it still wasn't enough.

Even when I pushed her down hard, hilting inside her in one brutal thrust. Even when we exploded together, it still wasn't enough.

The waves of climax had barely stopped when I lifted her off my still-hard cock. I left the tub, water pouring from my body to soak the floor. I ignored it to snatch a couple of towels from the cabinet and lay them out in front of me.

"Come on," I rasped, reaching for her.

Abby looked from my dark red cock to my shaking hand and stood. I helped her out of the tub, laid her down on the towels. Forced her legs apart with my shoulders. Only her taste in my mouth could satisfy the roaring inside me, the craving that burned me from the inside out despite the orgasm I'd just had. The same craving that told me the fucking end wasn't anywhere in sight. I would drown myself in her every way I could, wipe out every part of who I was except the part that belonged to her. Only then could I find some relief.

Chest heaving, cock throbbing, I spread Abby's lips wide and gripped her clit with my teeth.

"Levi?"

The breathless edge of fear and need that saturated her voice made me feel like He-man.

Stronger than any gun or knife or skill I'd ever learned on the street. Stronger than literally holding a man's life in my hands—and sometimes taking it. None of that even came close to what she did to me, and when I licked across her opening, her cream on my tongue was literally the icing on that cake. Power and pleasure filled me as I thrust my tongue deep, gathering more, sucking her clit into my mouth and nursing it to the chant of my name on her lips.

Abby lifted her knees back and out, giving me complete access. Her hands gripped my head tight, pulling my hair as she forced me closer. "Levi, please!"

I ate her out, desperate to gorge myself. Only when a flood of arousal met my tongue, signaling her impending orgasm, did I pull myself away.

I was inside her before my next heartbeat.

I have no idea when Abby peaked. All I knew was the violent need to thrust, to invade. To take. Over and over I drove inside her, finding exactly what I'd hoped for: an ocean of pleasure to drown myself in. My spine tingled, my balls drew up, and after an agony of waiting, my come exploded deep. Claiming her. Marking her in the basest way possible.

And finally, *finally* allowing the peace I hungered for to fill me.

Chapter Twelve

"We really have to stop meeting like this," Eli said as we walked out of the bedroom the next morning.

Abby chuckled. "Better than meeting some other ways."

True enough. Abby was used to my brothers enough to know they could show up at any time, so she never left any bedroom without full coverage. Today that meant a pair of leggings and one of my T-shirts. Only problem was, seeing her in my clothes just made me want to take them back off.

But we had work to do. Unfortunately.

Remi sat at the kitchen table, glowering into his cup of coffee. No breakfast, I guessed. I seriously had to have a talk with him. Whoever had pissed in his cornflakes needed to die so my brother could get back to his normal self.

The self that made something of a reappearance when Abby wandered toward the coffeepot.

"Don't do that, Abby. Have a seat," he said, standing. "I'll get it."

Abby gave him a smile and sat at the table. I rolled my eyes before opening the fridge in search of food.

"I'll do a grocery run today," Eli said, watching as I pulled a box of waffles from the freezer.

"I'll start a list," Abby volunteered.

Was this what it would be like if Abby and I lived together? All of us falling into a pattern, each with their own roles? My brothers and I had been our own self-enclosed unit for so long, but every time Abby was with us, she fit naturally into the mix. No fussing, no friction. Well, except between me and Remi. But having Abby involved gave me a weird sense of déjà vu, one I couldn't place—I had very few memories of my family's time before, when a woman had been a part of us, and yet Abby just felt right.

When Abby and I had dug into our waffles, a cup of coffee at each of our elbows, Abby's with the perfect amount of cream and sugar, just as she liked it—I was beginning to think my brother was doing this for no other reason than to piss me off, really—Eli cleared his throat.

"We need a confab."

Of course we did. I filled Remi in on what went down yesterday at our former warehouse. We were going to start running low on safe houses at this rate.

"Want to tell us how you found the bastards before they headed our way?" he asked.

Three pairs of eyes turned toward me.

I cleared my throat. "I was out at the mansion."

Two pairs of eyes dropped to the table.

"The mansion?" Abby asked.

"Where we grew up." I found myself staring at my plate and forced myself to look up. "The home we lived in with our parents was…ostentatious."

Abby raised an eyebrow. "So we have more in common than I knew, huh?"

Way more. But that was a discussion for another day. "Turns out the place isn't empty," I said instead of answering her question. "Rathlin is definitely involved; I saw him there, along with a small army of mercenaries. They're on to something big."

"But why?" Remi asked. "It's an inheritance. Sure, it's probably a shitload of money. And granted, they—whoever *they* is—seem to know they aren't dealing with your ordinary targets. But an army? To get rid of one man?"

"Three men," I pointed out. "The inheritance will go to any next of kin, so despite the fact that it's my birthday this seems to hinge on, all of us have to disappear."

"Still," Abby said, "Remi is right. Chadwick is rich in his own right. An old-money lawyer like that, who's been around for decades and only takes high-profile clients? He's not hurting. Men like that can always pad their bank accounts, but to hire an army? That's almost more outlay then it's worth, right?"

"The trust has been sitting for nineteen years, eleven since Amos died," Eli said.

"But even at that rate of interest, it seems excessive." Abby shrugged. "My dad was running for governor and had serious enemies, and he didn't hire an army."

"Our friend yesterday said Chadwick wasn't the one running the show," Eli pointed out. "I've been thinking about that," I said. "I did see someone with Chadwick on the doorstep, but I couldn't get a good look. Might be his partner. At minimum the man is involved somehow. If we could get some surveillance, a photo, maybe we could find out."

"Which makes even less sense." Remi tipped his coffee cup back and forth. "Now he's splitting the money. That's even less reward for more expense."

All of us fell silent, considering the angles.

"I don't think this is just about money," I said.

"When is it ever not about money?" Remi asked.

I shifted on the hard wooden seat. "The man yesterday asked if we'd read the trust. There something we're missing here. And I think we'll know what if we can get a copy of it." I cocked my head at Eli. "Would that be a matter of public record?"

"The wills certainly would be." His eyes glazed over like he was already deep in the wormhole of the Internet, working his magic. "They might not hold the details of the trust, but they could point us in the right direction. Certainly tell us who controls the assets. Even if the accounts have changed hands since then, it would give us a starting point."

For a moment I fell back in time, to that night I'd snatched my brothers from their beds, handed them tiny backpacks full of clothes and the little bit of packaged food I could find without drawing attention to myself, and helped them out a downstairs window of the mansion. What would've happened if I hadn't taken them and run? If I'd stayed under my uncle's thumb long enough to understand what had been at stake. Would I already know the secrets he'd hidden from us? Or would we have ended up as dead as my parents before we'd become a threat to his plans? He'd obviously not been worried about any threats when I'd returned at eighteen—I'd managed to bypass security and get his fat neck in my hands before he'd had even an inkling of danger.

Which also meant he'd had no time to hide anything.

"How much do you think Chadwick knows about how Amos operated?" I asked, not really looking for an answer, more thinking aloud.

Eli narrowed his eyes, obviously thinking too. "What do you mean?"

"The safe," Remi said.

I nodded. As boys we'd played in my father's office every afternoon while he worked. We'd all seen him open the hidden safe behind the bookcase in that room. "Would he know about it?"

"Probably." Remi contemplated the cup in his hands for a moment. "All these years with unrestricted access, I'm pretty sure Chadwick has been through every inch of the house."

"Or whoever he's partnered up with. They likely keep their own valuables in that safe," Eli pointed out.

"Getting to it would not be easy," I said despite the way anticipation thrummed in my veins. I'd like nothing better than to sneak behind enemy lines right beneath Chadwick's nose. "Rathlin's there."

"And Chadwick's ghost partner," Eli said.

"And there's the possibility that they've added another safe, replaced that one, changed the code…" Remi shrugged.

"It would probably be much easier to break into Chadwick's law office," Abby interjected.

We all turned to stare at her. She gave a little laugh as she stood, empty plate and cup in hand. "Men. Always making things more complicated."

I felt a smile tug at my lips despite myself. "Smart-ass."

Abby winked. "I'll go take a shower and leave you all to your planning."

The room was silent until the bedroom door clicked shut.

"She forgets this isn't a friendly game of cat-and-mouse," Remi said grimly. "They're out to make us disappear. Her too."

Because she was a part of us now. Forever linked and forever in danger. Because of me.

"She lost her home and almost lost her life a few days ago," I reminded him. "She knows exactly what's at stake."

"Does she?"

I went cold, my body tensing against the sudden need to pound his teeth in. "Since she's lost a lot more than you so far, I'd say yeah, she does."

"And whose fault is that?"

My chair screeched as I shoved to my feet. Remi didn't retreat when I leaned over the table, getting right in his face, but I could see a spark of something in his eyes, something I'd have to think about later. "I don't care what your deal is, brother, but if you don't stop with the dickhead comments, I'll feed them to you with my fist. Am I clear?"

A red flush rose up Remi's neck. "Gonna take me out to the woodshed, big brother?"

"You bet your ass I will," I bit out between clenched teeth.

Eli cleared his throat. "Let's get the plans settled first."

It took several deep breaths before I could make myself straighten. For myself, I didn't care. We'd had rough patches, beat each other up, and come out the other side stronger than ever. But whether his comments were aimed at Abby or just my role in this relationship, they would hurt her if she overheard.

And I was too damn crazy trying to figure this stuff out to put up with his shit. "Fine." I crossed my arms over my chest. "There is zero chance of remote surveillance on the mansion as is; it's too far off the grid for street cameras. And no way has Rathlin not secured their internal monitoring against outside access."

"True." Eli stood from the table and walked toward his temporary computer setup. "Where did you observe from yesterday?"

"The tree house."

"No way. Really?" Eli grinned like I'd handed him a puppy. "It's still there?"

"You were like seven," Remi pointed out. "How can you remember that?"

Eli shrugged, burying his head in the bags of equipment. "Nine. And I just do." After some shuffling, he straightened, a large box in his hand. "I think I have the answer to our eye problem, though." He started a pile, adding some cables and what looked like a battery pack. A remote camera. "I'll head out and set this up."

"Uh, you will not." No way in hell. Eli was nowhere near as familiar with the area as I was.

He gave me a get-real look. "You know, I have paid attention all these years. I'm not an idiot. Besides, if the system goes wonky, can you troubleshoot it?"

Fuck no. That's why he was the electronics expert.

Resignation settled on my shoulders, but it didn't dampen my tension. My job was to keep them out of danger, not put them in it. "I don't like it."

"I do," Eli threw over his shoulder as he packed the equipment into a bag. "I set up; Remi watches."

Remi groaned.

"Hours of entertainment for my dickhead bro. How could I not like that?" Eli's grin turned evil.

"Great. Thanks," Remi said.

"No problem." Eli clapped him on the shoulder on his way to the door. "Besides, this gives Levi a chance for that ass chewing you were due. It's a win-win all around."

"Then you're on your own when it comes to the research on Chadwick and the wills," Remi warned before Eli could leave. "My ass will be too sore to sit in a chair."

I'd make sure of it.

Eli shook his head. "Bro, I have a feeling that by the time I get back, more than your ass will be too sore to use. Have fun!"

After a wave he closed the door behind him. Remi slumped, his gaze stuck on the exit. When I didn't start in on him, he finally turned to meet my stare.

"If you don't want him to be right," I said, steel threading my words, "I suggest you tell me what the hell is going on with you. Now."

Chapter Thirteen

"None of your damn business."

The words were belligerent, but the tone… There was that something again. It sounded suspiciously like defeat.

"Remi…" Fuck. I hated this. I was the only father they truly remembered, but my dad—he'd been a good man. The best. I didn't want to know how he'd feel about what I did for a living, what I'd drawn Remi and Eli into. Some of his lessons, his morals had stuck with me. That's why I was so careful about the jobs I took. But the rest…

I didn't know how to do this part of who I was.

"Just tell me, bro."

His gaze drifted to the hall Abby had disappeared down. "It's a woman."

My heart literally seized. "Abby?"

"No!"

Relief deflated me quickly. So Abby reminded him of the woman he wanted. Or of what he wanted to have.

I watched him carefully as the pieces came together in my mind. "You won't let yourself have her."

"Fuck no."

Not a surprise. Look at where I was coming from. But I had to ask… "Why not?"

"Take a look around, Levi. Why would I put her through all this?"

I couldn't agree with him more, though I didn't say it aloud. I wanted far more for my brothers—and Abby; especially for Abby—than I'd ever wanted for myself.

"My and Abby's problems stem from the people around us, circumstances, not necessarily who we are." *Which is why her house is a pile of fucking charcoal—because of the people in my past.*

"Then run away," Remi said. "Leave all this behind."

"I can't." Even if I could, I wouldn't. My brothers might be adults, but they were still mine to protect.

"Why not? A couple of fake IDs, some disguises and you could be on your way to the Caribbean by nightfall with no way to track you."

I ground my teeth together, dropped my gaze to the shiny tabletop.

"But you won't, will you?"

"I should. Likely it would be the best way to keep Abby safe. That wouldn't protect you or Eli from whoever Chadwick is working for. With." I waved a hand vaguely. "Whatever."

"That's not the only reason and you know it."

I took a deep breath and met Remi's gold eyes. "You're right." Nathaniel Agozi's sense of justice—and the injustice of his and Miriam's deaths—would never let me walk away. Amos might have pulled the trigger, but it had led to this, to someone else trying to kill for their money. I couldn't let them go free, even to keep the woman I loved safe.

"I can't walk away either," Remi said. "This"—he flung his arms wide—"is who I am. It's all I know.

I might try, for her, but I would only take it with me. And possibly destroy her in the process."

Just like I had Abby. And I didn't just mean her house. She wanted all of me, but I was too fractured to give her that. Too scarred at my very core.

Remi was watching me. "Now you get it."

"I do, brother." And I had no idea what to do about it, for either of us.

Remi's fists went tight, his knuckles paling at the force. "I would rather never have her than to put her through hell."

"Abby's life isn't hell," I argued. It wasn't great at the moment, but I couldn't deny the impulse to defend her, defend us.

"But she's not totally yours, is she? She's in limbo. And believe me," Remi said grimly, "that's hell for a woman."

"What else can I give her?"

Remi shook his head. "That's exactly my point. She'd be happier, better off without you. But now that you've started with her, she can't free herself."

"That's my choice to make, don't you think, Remi?"

We both startled at Abby's voice, like two guilty boys raiding the cookie jar. Abby moved into the room, her pajamas replaced with jeans and a light sweater, her red hair still wet and pushed back from her face. She looked so young like this that I sometimes felt like the pervert she'd jokingly named me last night.

And the way my heart squeezed said it didn't matter. I'd rather be labeled a pervert than be lost to her forever.

"That's where you're wrong, little sis."

Because even Remi knew, fighting or not, that Abby was a permanent part of my life now. I could never let her go.

"Your life would be far better if he'd never walked back into it," Remi was saying. "If you'd been allowed to continue on the safe path and never got pulled over to the dark side."

Abby rested her elbows on the tall back of a dining room chair and leaned in, a sudden flush of anger turning her creamy skin pink. "Let me tell you something, *bro*—I've lived on the 'safe path' since I was born with a silver spoon in my mouth. And you want to know what it got me? Not a damn moment of actual safety. My mother was murdered and buried in concrete before I ever got the chance to remember her. My stepmother was murdered by a cut brake line. I lived with a man who abused and manipulated me with every breath I took. I was never safe. I didn't know what safe was.

"Until I walked into Levi's arms. That's the only safety I've ever known. And it's worth anything I have to give up to keep it."

"Then why try to walk away from me, Abby?"

This wasn't a conversation we should be having in front of Remi, but I couldn't stop myself from asking. Couldn't hold back the pain of the hole she'd ripped in my heart. We'd been too busy trying to figure out who was trying to kill us to think about anything else, but even when I'd had her in bed, when I'd been inside her, I couldn't forget that she'd wanted to leave.

"Because…what you were doing to me is only a little less torturous than what Remi is doing himself," she said. Straightening up, she met my eyes.

"Remi refuses to try in the first place. You're braver than that; you've at least tried to give me some semblance of what I want. What I need."

"But?"

Her frown said she wasn't sure how to explain it in a way I'd understand. I wasn't sure that was even possible. Wrapping my head around anything that risked Abby's safety probably wasn't going to happen.

"It's like offering a starving man a bite of the best food you could possibly conjure," she finally said. "And then refusing to give him any more. There isn't much he wouldn't give up to finally feel satisfied. At peace."

"He doesn't have much to give up. He's starving," Remi pointed out.

"Shut up, dumbass."

I couldn't help grinning at Abby's comeback. For never having had any siblings, she handled mine with ease.

Seeing them suffer her lack of patience, and not just me, was a bonus.

"The point is, all you're focused on is what she might have to give up. And I'm here to tell you that, for the right woman, it's all about what she would gain."

Remi stood. "She's not you, Abby. And while you may volunteer for this gig, I won't let her do the same."

Abby's eyes went sad as she watched him walk out the door. I felt for him, I truly did. But I also understood him in a way she never would. As men raised to protect, letting someone we loved walk knowingly into hardship, much less danger, was like asking us to sever our own tongue with a dull blade. Almost impossible.

Although having Abby say she wanted to leave me had sharpened the blade a good bit.

"Like denying a starving man, huh?"

Abby turned to me. Her arms came up, hugging her middle. Holding herself together, or protecting her vulnerable parts?

She shrugged. "Yeah."

I drew up the visceral memory of her cream on my tongue last night, her muscles strangling my cock. "I wasn't denying you last night."

She sighed. "This is not about sex, Levi."

Only a woman could use that tone of voice when denying the power of sex—dismissive, impatient.

I laughed. "Not all about sex."

When I started a slow stalk through the kitchen, she retreated into the living area, behind the couch. "Aren't we going to talk about this?" She swallowed hard. "About us?"

I let her see exactly what I wanted when her gaze met mine. "I'd rather do that once you're in your safe place, little bird."

She ducked her head, but not before I caught the shy, pleased smile on her face, the need in those hazel eyes. "Oh."

"Yeah," I said as I scooped her into my arms. "Oh."

I settled on the couch, Abby turned sideways on my lap so her legs rested on the cushions, her back against the arm. I wrapped a hand around her hip and pulled her tight against my chest. She shifted her ass, getting comfortable and—added bonus—waking up my cock. Her palm rested on my heart as if it belonged there, speeding up my pulse…because it did belong there, and always would.

"You want to leave me." I whispered the words into her hair, my heart suddenly galloping for a whole different reason.

Her fingers tightened, twisting into my shirt. "I never wanted to, Levi. I said I have to."

And I'd immediately jumped into dominant caveman mode: *Me, boss. You, stay.* This time I wanted—I needed—a different answer than I'd received before. "Why?"

"Because I'm starving," she said simply. And no, she didn't mean sex; I understood that, Neanderthal animal or not.

I let out a deep, heavy breath, laid my forehead against her hair. "I don't know how to be what you want me to be and also who I am, Abby. I'm not normal; I never will be."

"What's normal?"

I closed my eyes. "What you had—a house, a car, school. Normal."

"Can't we find *our* normal?" she asked. "Together?"

The *no* almost left my lips. There was no difference between *normal* and *our normal*, was there? It was just normal and not. And life had put me firmly on the *not* side of that line, whether I wanted to be there or where she was.

But as we sat there, the tension in her body communicated itself to mine. The rigid muscles, the held breath, the tight grip on my shirt. And I knew, in that moment, that whatever I said next would determine if we came out of this conversation with any hope for a future. I could hold Abby's body hostage, but I couldn't force her to give me her heart. That, only she could give.

So what was it going to be?

I'm starving.

I nuzzled her hair, letting her sweet scent push my fears away for now. If only I could stay here forever.

"Our normal?" I asked, voice husky from the knot in my throat.

The pulse throbbing in her neck skipped a beat. "Our normal."

I didn't know if such a thing even existed. All I knew was that I couldn't give up without at least a good fucking try. Either that or cut out my heart, because I wouldn't need the damn thing if she walked away.

"Okay." I brushed my lips along the shell of her ear, down to that stumbling, striking pulse. "Okay, little bird."

Chapter Fourteen

When Remi ducked his head cautiously back into the safe house, we got up and got to work. A basic search of county records told us that anything older than ten years wasn't archived online. We would need to go down to the courthouse to see my parents' wills. The idea of holding the papers in my hand, of seeing my parents' final wishes in the flesh, sent nausea roiling through me, but I got dressed anyway, letting Abby's hand in mine steady me as we headed downtown.

Leaving the SUV without a weapon left me feeling naked, but Remi would be observing via security cameras, at least outside. I wasn't naive enough to believe no one could get a weapon into the courthouse—or steal one from law enforcement inside—but I'd have to trust other skills today.

With Abby walking beside me, I wasn't happy accepting that.

Downtown was bustling at midmorning. Court was in session, lawyers and police officers everywhere, everyday citizens visiting the licensing and business departments. In the basement it was much quieter; not many people came to scrounge through dusty paper memories, apparently. The lady behind the counter eyed me up and down, a mix of dismay and something I thought might be reluctant appreciation in her gaze as it settled on the vee of my T-shirt and the hint of ink it revealed. Her lips tightened into a thin, prim line, her beehive hair swaying as she turned to Abby.

"May I help you, dear?"

With archives or with getting away from your scary boyfriend? I fought to hold back a smile as the thought echoed in my head.

The amusement in Abby's eyes made them sparkle—she'd caught the woman's reaction too. "Yes." She retrieved a paper from her pocket with my parents' names written on it. "We were hoping to see the records regarding the last will and testaments of these individuals."

The woman glanced at the paper, her brow furrowed. "Do you know the dates of death?"

Abby gave it, and the beehive bobbed this time as the woman nodded. After retrieving a pencil from the depths of hair behind her ear, the clerk wrote down the date. "This should not be a problem. If you and your"—she cleared her throat—"gentleman friend would like to have a seat, I'll retrieve the documents for you."

"Thank you."

I moved to a nearby bench, drawing Abby with me. Catching her eye, I mouthed, *Gentleman friend?*

Her choked-off giggle lightened the mood for the briefest moment.

"Nervous?" she asked quietly.

"Why would you ask that?" I wasn't nervous. Nerves weren't part of my MO. I had nerves of steel, always.

Abby wiggled her hand, and it was only then that I realized I was doing my best to crush her bones. With a muttered curse I let go. "I'm sorry."

She watched as I took her hand between mine and began kneading away the pain. "It's okay, you know."

It wasn't, but I didn't say so. What had happened to the man that was never fazed, who never felt anything? The man who'd done his job without emotion, simply because it needed to be done. Who knew in his head that he cared about his family, but never let the caring rule him. He was gone, and in his place was someone I feared might be too weak to protect them all.

Abby leaned close, sensing all that I wouldn't say despite trying to hold it back. Her warm breath whispered across my cheek to my ear. "Love isn't a weakness, Levi. You might have had to close some part of that off in order to survive, but you're not just surviving now. You're living. Lay down your sword for a little while and let yourself feel. Let yourself grieve."

My chest squeezed painfully. "Laying down my sword means running the risk of falling on it," I pointed out.

Abby shook her head, the familiar scent of vanilla and flowers surrounding me as her hair brushed my face. "Don't you want to remember what you're fighting for?" Her hand tightened around mine. "Isn't that what your parents would've wanted for you? For all of you?"

I couldn't answer that question. Parents wanted a lot for their kids, I was sure, but I barely remembered the time when hopes and dreams had lived in my parents' eyes. All I had was now.

"Miss?"

We looked up. The clerk had returned, her stacked hair shaking in agitation as she frowned across the counter. Abby stood and led the way over. "Yes?"

The frown deepened. "Unfortunately, I won't be able to help you."

"Oh." Abby was frowning now too. "Might I ask why?"

"Because these records are missing," the woman replied. "I can't say how or why. They would've been filed with us directly from the court. They should've been here all these years. But they aren't."

Something settled inside me. If we'd needed confirmation that we were on the right track, this was it.

"There are no records of the files being removed?" Abby asked. Did they even do that? I imagined a system like the library had, only for checking out files instead of books.

"I'm afraid not. Files aren't removable, though you can request copies. And I show no records of that either." The woman's agitation was clear, her perfectly ordered world thrown into disarray. "The only way to track them down now would likely be through the lawyer who filed them."

Abby met my gaze. We both knew how likely Chadwick was to hand over copies.

After thanking the lady, we exited the records office. "Now what?" Abby asked.

Good question. I wasn't sure. "B and E?" I suggested, only half kidding.

Abby focused on that half and elbowed me, but I caught the edge of worry on her face as I trailed her to the upper floor.

"We'll figure it out," I assured her. We walked into the rotunda entry of the courthouse, me slightly trailing behind.

Abby came to an abrupt halt in front of me.

"What—"

And then I saw him too. Alan Chadwick stood at the opposite end of the room, his back almost turned to us as he talked with another man in a suit. Another lawyer, most likely.

I grabbed Abby's arm. "Let's go."

But she pulled against my grip. "I have an idea," she said, the spark of determination in her eyes spelling trouble.

I growled, that look putting me on high alert. "Abby, no—"

But she was already walking toward him. And I was getting angrier with every step she took closer to my enemy.

"Mr. Chadwick!"

I almost did a double take. The Abby I knew was the real woman, not the plastic, professional hostess her father had forced her to become before I kidnapped her. That old Abby slid over her skin like a mask, making her more remote and yet somehow more friendly. Fake. It was so fucking wrong it made my skin crawl.

And then Chadwick turned around, his gaze searching. And met mine over Abby's shoulder.

Green looked good on him. At least from my perspective. I doubted he felt the same.

Good.

"Mr. Chadwick," Abby said again. "I hope you don't mind me interrupting."

The man standing with him gave us a nod, walking away with a promise to call later. Chadwick managed to push back his anxiety and blank his expression.

"I am sorry; do I know you?" he asked pleasantly enough.

Good one. I almost believed it.

"I'm Abigail Roslyn," she answered, sounding like she was in a tea parlor rather than facing down a man who'd ordered her murder, the destruction of her house. "I was a longtime client of Lance Heinz, as was my father."

"Of course, of course." He extended his hand, and I clamped down tight on the instinct to crush it before he could make contact with my woman.

"I wanted to express my condolences," Abby said, extricating herself from his touch quickly yet politely. It was a good thing she possessed an abundance of social skills; from the way Chadwick kept glancing at me and the rigid feel of my face, I had basically zero social skills on display.

Which was just the way I liked it.

"Losing a partner of so many years must be difficult," she was saying. "I'm not sure if you remember, but we've met a couple of times. When I was much younger."

"Of course." It seemed to be the only response he could give. That and a smile that was all teeth. "How could I forget such a lovely young woman?"

I managed to keep the growl in my chest right where it was. Barely.

"Lance was a great fan of your father's," Chadwick finally managed to get out.

"Yes, he contacted me recently. About some accounts I needed to look over. Unfortunately I wasn't able to meet with him about them before he died."

I gritted my teeth.

"Whom might I speak with now that he has passed?" she asked.

Over my dead body, I wanted to say but didn't. Those accounts didn't exist; we'd determined that much. And Chadwick would know that as well as we did. She was baiting the tiger, looking for a slipup.

Too bad for her that the animal snarling silently behind her had every intention of punishing her for putting herself in danger later. The rest of me waited avidly for Chadwick's response, damn it.

"Ah." He glanced between the two of us, never quite meeting my eyes, but I didn't think that was wholly nerves. No, he knew he wouldn't be able to hide from me if I was able to look into his eyes. "As you can imagine, the suddenness of my partner's death has left things in a bit of chaos. Manassas and I are doing what we can to take up the slack, but it will be a few weeks before we will have everything in order."

A few weeks as in, right after my thirtieth birthday. It hadn't escaped my notice that Chadwick hadn't questioned who I was, nor introduced himself.

Was Manassas the other man I'd seen at the mansion? I made a mental note to look him up when we got back to the safe house.

"The way Lance talked, the matter was somewhat urgent," Abby pointed out. "Perhaps I should check in with the accountant instead."

A sheen of sweat popped up along Chadwick's brow, but I had to hand it to him—he could bullshit as well as any lawyer I'd ever met. "Of course. That might be fastest. Have them make an appointment with my office should there be any questions."

There would definitely be questions on nonexistent accounts. We all knew that.

"Thank you," Abby said. "I'll do that. Again, my condolences."

She turned to leave. There was a moment, barely noticeable, when Chadwick and I stood face-to-face, no one between us. Just two killers measuring each other up. And that's what he was. He might not have pulled the trigger on my parents, might not have thrown the Molotov cocktails himself, but Chadwick was responsible, and he knew it. I knew it.

And in that single moment, I let him see deep into me—the determination, the power, the ferocious need to hold his neck in my hands and snap it like a twig.

I was coming for him, and he could hire a thousand mercenaries, but they wouldn't be able to stop me. He was a dead man walking, and in that moment, he knew it.

Chapter Fifteen

"You're not going to spank me, Levi. Forget about it."

"Sounds kinky," Eli joked as Abby and I walked through the door to the safe house. "You think you know someone…"

"You're going to want to spank her too." My heart still hadn't slowed after the shock of having her waltz up to Alan Chadwick and carry on an all-but-threatening conversation as if she had balls the size of grenades.

"Sounds even kinkier," Eli said.

I leveled my meanest look on him. "She confronted Chadwick, right there in the courthouse."

"What?"

Even Remi got in on that one. Both of my brothers turned from their computers, eyes wide, mouths hanging open. Both gradually narrowed glares on Abby as my words sank in.

"Damn right she needs a spanking," Remi said.

"Try it and die, douchebag." Abby threw her purse onto a chair and went to the fridge to retrieve a bottle of water. "He needed to know we were on to him. And that we weren't afraid."

"He definitely knows," I said.

Eli cocked his head. "The question is, what's he going to do about it now?"

"With any luck after the death glare Levi gave him, he'll fall back and regroup." Abby chugged half the bottle, all while eyeing me with satisfaction.

I stepped into her space, letting my death glare out the slightest bit. "Your ass is still mine, little bird," I said so only she could hear.

Abby was getting too used to me; there wasn't even a hint of cowering. Just a saucy wink that made me want to spank her all the more. "You wish."

I did. But we could discuss kinky sex another time. Right now—

A distinctive ring sounded from the vicinity of the computers—the burner phone I'd only used with Detective Bryant. Eli passed it to me quickly.

"Agozi."

"It's Bryant."

From the first word I knew something was up. The rush in his voice, the strain. I pulled the phone away from my ear and switched it to speaker. "What's wrong?"

"I need to meet with you."

His voice sounded even worse as it echoed through the room. The four of us exchanged identical frowns. "At the station?"

"No. Anywhere but there, actually."

"What the hell is going on, Bryant? Just spill it."

"My partner is in critical condition, that's what's going on," he bit out. "I was almost fucking next. And I'll be damned if I die over leads on what should've been a simple arson case. Is that enough for you?"

A small sound escaped Abby—concern. I felt it too. I didn't trust anyone but family, but Bryant had warned us about Chadwick. That counted for something. "Tell me what happened."

"I can't say anything more. Just meet me. Someplace secure."

I ran through a list of options in my head, finally settling on an abandoned convenience store on the edge of town that we'd used before. "Two hours." We could wait till dark gave us the advantage, give ourselves time to put backup in place.

A gruff laugh, followed by a cough, came through. "In two hours I'll be unconscious. They don't let you walk away from a gunshot wound without doping you up. I managed to keep it to a minimum, but this hurts like hell and I'm no martyr."

That explained the sound of his voice. Pain and painkillers. I raised an eyebrow at my brothers.

There are times when, despite all outward appearances, you have to trust your gut. My gut said Bryant was clean. And if he and his partner had been targeted...

Eli and Remi both nodded.

"Twenty minutes then." I gave Bryant the address.

"I'll be there."

The line went dead in my ear. I turned to Remi. "Suit up."

He didn't question me. Neither did Eli when I asked him to stay with Abby. It was Abby who protested.

I gathered my things. "You're not going."

"But—"

"Here, little sis." Eli handed her an earpiece just like the one I'd slipped into my ear. "Now you can hear everything as it happens, talk to him if you need to. And Levi can go in undistracted."

Her body relaxed. It was the not knowing that got to her. I understood, but no fucking way was I allowing her to walk into danger.

I dropped Remi off a couple miles south of our target. He would come in on foot, keeping an eye out for anyone who shouldn't be in the area, anyone showing too much interest in our location. There were no high buildings and very little cover around, so we should be safe from snipers. I pulled the SUV up behind the station, close to a heavy blue dumpster, and got out.

And immediately heard the coughing breath of Bryant nearby. The sound wasn't wet, but the man wasn't breathing normally either.

I pulled my gun, leaving it down by my thigh in case my gut was wrong. The smell of garbage filled my nose as I rounded the dumpster. "Bryant."

The detective slouched against the building, his hearty olive skin showing a sickly undertone that confirmed the pain he was in. A bulky pad distorted the right shoulder of his shirt. I jerked my chin toward it. "Through and through?"

"Luckily. Ticker's too old to be happy about the trauma, but I'll manage." Bryant's gaze dropped to my weapon. "You don't need that. My gun hand ain't no good right now anyway. But I'm not here to take you out; I'm here to warn you."

"Where's your car?"

"Cab." He shrugged, then grunted in pain. "Didn't have my car at the hospital. Had him drop me off a couple blocks over."

Covering his tracks. Good. I squatted down in front of him. "Your partner?"

Bryant swallowed, the sound a dry click in the quiet. "Benny took one to the throat. Touch and go. He has a wife and kids." Bryant glared up at me. "I'm going to get the bastards who did this."

And I'd help him. I glanced up to see Remi doing a slow jog across the street toward us. With a flick of my fingers, I signaled him over. When I turned back to Bryant, he was swaying against the concrete wall.

"Let's get you in the SUV," I said. Better protection. Besides, if he thought he was going to wait for another cab, he was sorely mistaken. We'd take him wherever he needed to go.

He weaved his way to the vehicle, pulling open the back door to crawl onto the bench seat. "Son of a bitch," he bit out as his shoulder hit the cushions.

"Just a scratch." I settled onto the seat next to him, Remi taking the driver's seat.

"I'm fifty-three years old," Bryant said grumpily. "At my age a scratch can kill me."

"What the hell happened?" Remi asked, turning to give Bryant a close look.

The detective returned the favor. "You're one of the brothers, aren't ya? Can't miss that resemblance."

Remi scowled and kept his mouth shut.

Bryant shook his head. "Drive-by," he croaked. Then cleared his throat. "A couple blocks from that lawyer's office. Chadwick. The one in charge of your dad's estate. We were going to check out the will and trust."

My narrowed eyes met Remi's.

"Black SUV came out of nowhere. No plates. I caught that much as I hit the pavement." Bryant shrugged his left shoulder. "After that I was too busy yelling into the phone and keeping pressure on Benny so he didn't bleed out in front of me.

"I knew it couldn't be a coincidence. The fire targeted you and your girl. My partner and I were asking questions about your parents' estate, and ten minutes after we leave the squad room, where four or five people know who we're going to question, we get gunned down? I'm not a patrol officer facing gangbangers every day; no way was this a coincidence," he repeated.

"It's too much like the bank," Remi said.

It was.

"What bank?" Bryant asked.

I noticed him swaying a bit, his eyes glazing even more—pain meds getting the better of him—but didn't mention it. "We had a similar incident earlier this week, before the fire. At a meeting set up by Abby's lawyer, Lance Heinz."

"The one who's dead?"

"Yeah, that one."

Bryant's brow furrowed. "Definitely not a coincidence, then. Is it possible he knew you and Abby were connected somehow? Were you dating before her father died?"

The likelihood that Heinz had known, had possibly been involved in hiring me in the first place, was high. And after Roslyn had tracked me down through Remi, well, we hadn't had the option of disguises in the hospital. Facial recognition on my brother could've given them enough to go on.

"Anything's possible." And the chances were high that the two lawyers had somehow compared notes and made connections.

And because of those connections, a cop was lying in the hospital, knocking at death's door.

"Have you ever heard of Hacr Technologies?" Bryant asked.

The name was vaguely familiar, but I couldn't place it. I glanced at Remi, who shook his head.

"It was our father's tech company," Eli said in my ear, startling me. I'd known our father was involved in communications research, but had never felt the need to investigate further. Obviously Eli had.

When I passed the information along, Bryant nodded. "Haven't seen the paperwork yet, but I do know your dad founded the company and was a majority shareholder. Other than his inheritance from his father, there's nothing else in his background that might account for whatever the hell is going on here." Bryant shifted in his seat, and blood drained from his face. He needed to get out of here and get more pain meds soon. "My uneducated guess is something in the trust involves that company."

I'd say his uneducated guess was right based on my gut. But I knew Remi and Eli would be researching the second we got back. Hell, Eli was probably already on the computer, digging.

Bryant's faded blue eyes locked with mine, his intensity burning bright despite the wearing of age. "They want to make whatever this is go away. They came after you, and now they've come after me. They want it all to die—the questions, the trust, everything connected with your name. They can't keep the contents of the trust secret unless you and anyone else who knows about you are gone. It's the only way to protect whatever it is they want."

I wasn't worried about me, or even my brothers, really. Rathlin's army be damned; Chadwick wouldn't be able to get to us, not now that we knew what we were up against. But if Bryant's partner died? I might be an assassin, but I still had a conscience. I'd carry that stain forever.

"The question is, how do we stop them from going after anyone else?"

"The only person with access to the intel we need is trying to kill us," Remi pointed out. "It's hard to put the puzzle pieces together without the pieces."

"Right." Silence settled between us until I heard a click in my ear, then Abby's voice.

"Levi?"

"What?"

I heard some rustling like she was fidgeting in her seat. Then, "They want anyone who knows you're alive to disappear, right?"

"Right."

"Then we make sure as many people know your name as we possibly can," she said, a lilt to the words that told me she was enjoying the thought of thwarting our enemies. "They can't kill them all."

My eyes met Remi's, knowing he'd heard Abby's words too. The wicked smile that spread across his face told me all I needed to know. "That's the best idea I've heard in years. Let's make you a celebrity, brother."

Oh fuck no.

Chapter Sixteen

"Where the fuck did you find this thing?"

The tux fit me perfectly, damn it. I'd heard them called monkey suits, and at this moment, squirming in the snug pants and tugging at the tight collar of the dress shirt while I stared with true fear at the confining jacket lying on the bed, I understood why. Give me a tactical vest, fatigues, and a hundred-pound pack of equipment any day—this was the real torture.

Abby seemed to be enjoying my discomfort a little too much as we stood before the warped mirror in the safe-house bedroom. "Charlotte."

Charlotte again? Who was this woman?

Who cared? Right now I hated her guts.

"Who—"

My woman smoothed her hands down my chest, a small grin playing on her lips. "A friend."

"Since when do you have friends?"

Not what I'd meant to say, but the glare Abby shot my way convinced me to keep any attempts at explaining behind my lips.

"I do have friends. You'd know that if—"

I kissed her hard on the mouth. "I know; if I stuck around during the day."

"Right, dickhead," she said as she picked up the black bow tie lying on the bed. "I knew Charlotte before my dad…you know." She waved a hand vaguely, the ends of the tie swinging in the air. "A few months ago we reconnected. She founded a charity that assists low-income families in affording adoptions."

"Hmm." Sounded noble of her. I glanced down at the dress clothes and wondered if I needed a background check on this Charlotte. Or maybe we'd skip right to the torture considering she was the one who'd provided the monkey suit.

"You're pouting like a little boy forced to dress up for church."

"We were Jewish. We didn't go to church; we went to temple," I reminded her.

"Did you wear a yarmulke?"

I could hear it in her voice; she was imagining three stair-step boys with little black yarmulkes on their heads, following their parents into temple. My memories of that time were almost as rosy, so I wasn't sure if it truly had been rosy or I'd simply colored them that way after living on the streets, in the midst of violence.

"Of course we did."

"Then you're more than familiar with fashion over a comfort."

I groaned. I'd hated wearing the hat. Most kids did.

When she moved close, her hands brushing my neck to slide the bow tie under my collar, I took the opportunity to grip her hips and force her against me.

"You'll wrinkle," she protested, but her eyes didn't protest.

Fuck wrinkles. "I love your eyes."

Smooth palms slid along my cheeks, drawing me down until our foreheads met. I was so close I could see the individual blue and green and brown stripes in her irises. Close enough that I couldn't miss the flash of something uncertain as her gaze dropped to my mouth.

"Do you?" she asked.

I dug my fingertips in deep, grinding my semihard cock against the softness of her belly. "Of course I do." How could she doubt that?

Abby dropped her gaze to the tie, hiding her expression. "I want you to love more than just my eyes, Levi," she whispered.

My knee-jerk instinct was to force her head back, take her mouth in a long, hard, branding kiss, and not stop until we were both sweaty and sated. I didn't. That would be a way to hide, to keep the focus on sex and not being as naked before her as she'd just made herself before me. Abby deserved so much more.

Instead I took a long, deep breath, gathered my fucking courage, and transferred my grip to her neck, holding her still as I stared straight into those goddamn gorgeous eyes.

"I love you, little bird."

Her eyes went wide.

I leaned in until my lips brushed hers. "I love you. I have from the moment you stared up at me with those eyes and said yes when I asked you to dance."

"Before you kidnapped me?" she asked, one side of her mouth quirking up.

Maybe even before that. I had spent days watching her, learning her habits, waiting for just the right opportunity. I'd wanted her as much for me as I had for revenge by the time I approached her at the club that night we met. It would've been so easy to snatch her at any time, but I hadn't been able to resist the chance to take her to bed before I took her away from her life. Call me a bastard, but I'd needed her in a way I was only now beginning to understand. Only now that I'd realized I loved her.

It was Abby who kissed me then, soft and sweet and honest. The kind of honesty I'd tended to avoid before with fast, hard sex. Abby had taught me better; in the months we'd been together, she'd taught me that it truly was safe in her arms.

"Have you thought about what this means?" she asked as she went back to work on my bow tie. Like she needed a focus, which, granted, I could understand considering the confusing loops and tucks she was performing under my chin. But that wasn't why she was avoiding my eye. The question was anything but casual.

"That I love you?"

"No." She flipped me a glance of pure joy at the declaration, though. Did just saying *I love you* really mean that much to women? "That you'll be outing yourself to society."

The shudder that hit me couldn't be hidden. "Only because those are the circles Chadwick runs in. The circles that matter."

Abby laid her hands flat on my chest. "Those are also the circles that will know very quickly about your inheritance. Once you do this, you'll have no choice but to claim it. What is that going to mean to you? Your life? Your brothers' lives?"

The shudder was nothing compared to the surge of fear that hit me. Fear had been nonexistent in my life since I'd learned to use my fists. Abby was the only person on the planet that could make me afraid, and this step, necessary though it might be to protect everyone, could change our life together. Would she want to go back to what she'd known before, the glitz and glamour and wealth her father had been immersed in? Would she find someone else, someone more sophisticated, less ruthless? Would she still want me if I chose to continue the life I'd led up to now? I'd never known anything else, not really. Two-thirds of my life had been tied up in violence.

"I don't know," I said honestly. "I don't know what to expect, what I want."

A vee dug deep between her eyebrows. "But…?"

"But…not doing this would mean walking away from my parents, and I can't do that, not anymore. There are a hundred practical reasons to go public, but the one that really matters to me is making the past right. For them."

She kissed me again, but it wasn't soft or sweet this time. Apparently my woman had a thing for altruism.

"Explain to me again where we're going?" I asked when she released me. Tuxedo pants weren't exactly made to accommodate a screaming erection.

Abby stepped back, eyed my dilemma—which only made it worse—and snorted in amusement before turning her attention to my question. "The St. Mary's Sisters of Charity was the place that took my mother in when she ran away from home."

Abby's mother had escaped an abusive family as a teen, I knew, and been helped by the shelter here in the city to get on her feet. "So the charity dinner is for them?"

"Among others," she said. "It's an annual event that highlights charities for the homeless in the city. St. Mary's is honored every year."

"Why did they invite you when you aren't on the society circuit anymore?" Abby had lived quietly in her new home, far from the circles her father, then a gubernatorial candidate, had frequented. All she'd wanted was to go to school, have friends, get a job, have a boyfriend. Be normal.

My heart squeezed.

"Because when I sold Derek's mansion, I donated the money to them."

This time my heart stopped. That was millions of dollars.

"Why?" I choked out. "That money could've set you up for life."

Abby shrugged and handed me the black socks to go with the dress shoes she'd gotten me. "I'm already set for life with the inheritance. I didn't need it. If they could help someone else like they helped my mom…"

"So what you're saying is, all the focus will be on you as their special guest, and I just have to smile and look pretty?" Thank God.

Abby smirked like I'd known she would. "Your relief at that fact doesn't become you as a hit man."

"Are you kidding?" I shot her a sexy look from under my brows. "That's what us hit men do, fade into the background."

"You couldn't fade into the background if you tried. Get you into a roomful of women, especially in a tux"—a hungry growl left her—"and we're likely to have a stampede."

The strangest sense of pride hit me. I'd never given a fuck if I looked good unless I needed to for a job; all that mattered most of the time was being strong and capable. But Abby's gaze on me, her craving for me… Jesus, how did other men do this?

As I put on the stiff shoes, Abby moved to the emerald-green dress hanging on the door of the closet. When she dropped her robe, a visceral punch hit my stomach.

"Can I ask you something?"

"Sure," I said absently, my gaze on the side view of her breast as she reached for the dress.

"Why not just kill Chadwick?"

It was the simple solution, right? Get rid of him and our problem went away. He'd already killed two men that we knew of.

"Because he isn't the only one involved."

"So we follow him up the food chain?" She stepped into the circle of material spilling over the floor and pulled it slowly up her body.

"We have a good chance of doing that tonight, in fact." It was the second reason I'd agreed to do this, the first being to safeguard those around me.

"Will you kill him after?" She clutched the bodice to her generous breasts, small spaghetti straps tethering it at her shoulders.

I stomped my pants legs down as I stood, moving to stand behind Abby, reaching for the zipper of her dress. "Would it bother you if I did?" I finally asked, but it felt more like *could you accept who I am if I did?*

She raised her head, staring straight at me in the reflection of the mirror, and a savage light burned in her eyes. "It wouldn't bother me a damn bit."

My cock tightened all over again, at the sight of her, fierce with the need for vengeance, and at my own satisfaction. This was the woman for me, no doubt about it. The woman who, if I allowed her to, would accept me exactly as I was. All I had to do was let her in.

"Good," I said, letting the need for her roughen my voice. "You won't be disappointed then."

Chapter Seventeen

Why did it take so much more discipline not to tug at the tight bow tie around my throat than it did to wait patiently for a mark to walk into your trap? Because seriously, this fucking thing felt like it was strangling me.

"You look like someone has you in a choke hold," Abby whispered, her amusement plain.

"Feels like it too," I growled.

She reached up to smooth my collar. Oh yeah, she was definitely amused. I'd have to remind her of that later, when I punished her.

"Just remember to tell Charlotte thank you when we see her. She pulled off a miracle, whether you know it or not."

The mysterious Charlotte would be here tonight? "I'll definitely say something," I promised, just not what, exactly.

Abby snickered. She knew me too well—and accepted my rough edges better than I ever could the glamour. She was the miracle, not a tux.

How the hell had I found myself here in the first place? Following Abby up the marble steps of the city's largest museum as dozens of couples dressed just like us, only with far more diamonds, walked the same direction. It was surreal, nothing like the grit and grime I'd spent the last nineteen years immersed in.

And far too close to the times I remembered my parents going out in the evenings. Leaving us boys with a babysitter. This was their world, their people. And here I was, pretending I was worthy to enter the sacred space that had once been theirs.

"Abby!" A young woman in a neat nun's habit, hair buried beneath a black veil, rushed to meet us as we entered the lobby. Someone from St. Mary's, I presumed. "Thank you for coming."

"Thank you for inviting me, Sister Katherine."

The nun's warm smile stretched to encompass me. "There are cocktails being served in the reading room. May I show you the way?"

But Abby waved Sister Katherine on. "You have much more important things to attend to. We'll find it." She leaned in, exchanging a brief but heartfelt hug. "Will I see Margaret later?"

"She wouldn't miss seeing you," Sister Katherine said, then hurried off.

"Margaret?" I asked as we walked through the museum lobby.

"The head of St. Mary's." A hollow look filled her eyes before she blinked it away. "Margaret knew my mother for a short time."

I wanted to stop, to drag Abby to one side of the wide hall and kiss her until that look was a thing of the past, until pain was a distant memory. But I couldn't have what I wanted, not right now, not with the crowd surging around us. All these people made it difficult to determine threats, to position myself so I could protect Abby if I needed to. It kept me on alert, tense. I'd never had social niceties to begin with, but now… The men here might seem more civilized, but they knew a threat when they saw one, and gave me a wide berth.

The women were another matter altogether.

"I told you there might be a mob," Abby murmured as I handed her a glass of champagne from a passing tray.

Women in all directions were glancing our way, some covertly and some without an ounce of shyness about the hunger flaring in their eyes as they settled on me. I was tempted to suck back my entire glass but limited myself to a small sip; I didn't, however, resist the need to tug at my tie. "It's warm in here, isn't it?"

Abby chuckled.

To our right I caught sight of an older woman in a blue sequined gown, white hair gently curling around her head, gliding toward us, arms outstretched. Abby broke into a wide smile. "Mrs. Davenport, what a pleasure to see you again." She reached for the older woman's hand, real affection in her voice.

Nancy Davenport. A former governor's wife, and from what Abby had told me, the only one of her father's acquaintances to take a motherless girl under her wing when Abby first stepped into the role of her father's hostess.

"Darling Abby, it's so good to have you back with us." She enveloped Abby in a cloud of Chanel No. 5 and air-kisses.

"Oh, I'm not back, Mrs. Davenport," Abby assured her. "Simply a visit for my favorite charity."

"I know they find you a blessing, my dear." She leaned back, her faded green eyes seeming to take in every detail of Abby's face. "You're doing well."

A statement of fact, not a question. A soft smile answered her. "I am."

I held back the denial that wanted to escape me. How could Abby say that? She'd lost her home, someone was trying to kill us, and she was shackled to a man whose emotional growth had been stunted in childhood. It was amazing she was still sane.

And yet that smile didn't lie, nor did the hand that reached for mine.

Mrs. Davenport's gaze latched on to the move, then trailed up my chest to my face. "And who do we have here?" she cooed.

Red tinged Abby's cheeks, a soft blush that made me want to kiss her. I took Mrs. Davenport's hand instead, her papery skin soft against my calluses. "I'm Abby's boyfriend, ma'am. Levi Agozi."

Her eyes went wide. "My my my, you are a handsome one, aren't you?" She winked Abby's way. "You are one lucky girl, my dear. And deserve every moment of it."

"I believe I am the lucky one, Mrs. Davenport," I said and meant every word.

An actual twinkle lit the older woman's eyes. "Why you— Wait, did you say Agozi?"

"Yes."

Friendly speculation slid over me again. "Any relation to Nathaniel Agozi?"

My breath caught in my throat. "My father."

The words came out gruff, but I don't think Mrs. Davenport noticed. She was turning to scan the room, a light laugh escaping her. "That scamp! I can't believe Redding didn't tell me you were here." She turned back to us. "He knows how close I was to your dear mother." Her scrutiny this time was more personal. "How in the world did I miss it? You have your father's face. And definitely his looks."

"Redding?" Abby asked.

"Warren Redding. Head of Hacr Tech, you know."

Abby was shaking her head. "I don't think we've met."

"He knows you're here, of course?" Mrs. Davenport asked me. "He and your father were so close, but I had no idea he'd kept track of you."

I cleared my throat. "It's been a while."

Abby glanced at me. I slid my arm around her shoulders, warming the chill I could feel taking over her bare skin.

"Well, I'll give him a mouthful when I see him." Mrs. Davenport's attention was drawn to a side door, where a servant gestured for her. "I must see what's on fire before dinner can be served. Excuse me."

After hugging Abby one final time, the older woman disappeared toward the kitchen. Abby turned to me, a frantic look in her eyes. "How do we—"

My cell vibrated in my breast pocket. Abby paused as I pulled it out. The screen brightened when I tapped it, a notification for a text showing. I clicked it open.

"There you are, you bastard."

I showed Abby the picture Eli had sent as he listened in on our conversation through my earpiece. An older man, deep wrinkles framing his eyes and mouth, built like a bull, with thick, dark hair and eyebrows. Warren Redding.

Scrolling down, I scanned the bio Eli had attached. CEO of Hacr, appointed twenty years ago by the board, of which my father had been the majority shareholder. Head of research and development. Had he been my father's friend?

No, he couldn't be. Those shoulders and hair fit the man I'd seen on the mansion's doorstep. Redding was in my family's home; he was no do-gooder. This was our mastermind, and he was here. Tonight.

"Levi?"

"Hmm?"

I couldn't focus on anything but the sudden need to find Redding and slit his throat…until Abby's hand settled on the bare skin of my wrist. Her touch eased the bloodlust running through my veins. I met her eyes.

"Remember why we're here," she said quietly.

She was right; I knew that. I'd learned long ago not to go off half-cocked. Still… Maybe it was the realization that Redding must be in charge, maybe it was the direct connection to my father, I wasn't sure; I only knew this felt different. It felt…primal, inescapable, this need to protect what was mine.

But I couldn't give in.

A deep breath helped steady me as I absorbed the strength I needed through Abby's touch, her look, the total belief in me that shone in her eyes. Another lungful in, out, and I dredged up a measure of calm. We both knew that somewhere, walking around this room, was our enemy, but that wasn't our battle, not yet. "Ready."

She held on to me a moment longer, then slid her hand down to entwine our fingers. "Good. Let's go."

Chapter Eighteen

Everywhere we turned, there were diamonds and tuxes, champagne and caviar. Guests who hadn't blinked an eye at ten thousand a plate. And Abby seemed to know them all. She chatted effortlessly and smiled genuinely while I swept the room in constant search of our enemy. I should have been searching for a petite whirlwind that hit with the force of a hurricane.

"Abby!"

A tiny bundle of purple fabric swept into my woman's arms. My entire body went tight, my first instinct to pull the Kimber 9 mm from its spot at the small of my back to ward off the potential threat. Only Abby's hand landing on my arm, her soft touch reassuring me, stopped the movement.

"Charlotte!" She eased the woman back. One look at her face and I knew: this Charlotte mattered to her. Aside from Geneva, the older woman Abby visited who'd known her mother, this was the first person who'd come into Abby's life that she'd even mentioned, much less cared for.

I didn't like the green haze that filtered across my vision at the thought.

"Is this him?" Charlotte asked, dark gaze sweeping from my head to my feet and back again. "This is him."

The slight purr in her voice had my eyes narrowing.

Abby laughed. "It is." Snuggling closer to my side, she said, "Charlotte, this is the infamous Levi Agozi. Levi, my friend Charlotte Alexander."

I reached automatically for her hand, busy cataloging everything about her. Eli would be processing intel as soon as he heard her full name. I wanted everything, every detail. Any threat to Abby—

Delicate fingers slipped against my palm. "It's a pleasure to finally meet you, Levi." Charlotte dipped her head closer to Abby, her gaze still trained on me. "He's a bit fierce, isn't he?"

You have no idea.

I startled when the same words escaped Abby's mouth. The stares I'd received all night had barely registered beyond a vague impression of attention, but this woman knew Abby, had talked to her about me. What details had they shared? Had Abby told her what we did together? Who I really was?

No, Abby wouldn't reveal something so crucial to my safety and hers. But something in Charlotte's stare, the way she looked over my body, said she knew other things.

I dropped her hand, shifting uncomfortably, though I wasn't sure why.

The woman had a rich, throaty laugh that made you want to join in despite the fact that you weren't in on the joke. "I do believe that's a blush, isn't it?"

Abby winked my way. "I do believe it is."

For fuck's sake. Could we go back a few hours to when Abby had no close female friends?

And was I really that bastard, the one who didn't want her to be happy? The lightness in Abby's eyes right now, so different from when she'd looked to me earlier, worried about Redding, should have made me happy, not jealous.

For fuck's sake is right.

"Charlotte, it's a pleasure to meet a friend of Abby's. Thank you"—I tugged at my bow tie, cleared my throat—"for the tux."

The woman eyed me sympathetically now. "My father hates them too, but you're welcome. Anything for Abby."

Abby glanced up at me. "Charlotte and I knew each other back when…" Her smile faltered. "You know, way back when."

When she'd still been under her father's thumb.

"Thankfully both of us are in much better places now," Abby said.

"Places where we aren't bound by the dog-eat-dog rich girls' code and can actually choose friends of our own." Charlotte's soft voice rang with relief.

"Where's your fiancé?" Abby asked. "Is he here tonight? I was hoping to meet him finally."

Charlotte's smile hinted at strain. "He couldn't make it, I'm afraid. Business in DC."

"Of course."

Something in Abby's voice told me there was a story there, not that I should want to hear it. Abby concerned me, not other people. But there was something about the petite dynamo that had me wondering.

The women continued to talk, moving from the charities involved tonight to upcoming events to people they knew from years past. I listened, watched, and waited as the evening wore on, finding that the different parts of me clawed at each other—the assassin, the lover, the brother, all at war, all wanting control. They all coalesced when I caught sight of Warren Redding entering the ballroom when we walked in to dinner.

Abby saw him too; her arm, looped inside mine, went tight, and her step hitched.

"No worries, little bird." I wouldn't let there be, not for her. Worrying, and fixing that worry, those were my responsibilities.

"We're over here," Charlotte said, leading the way. Oblivious to the byplay following in her wake.

I slid my arm from Abby's and flattened my palm at the small of her back, letting my touch in such a sensitive place warm her as I guided her toward our seats at a table near the front. I had just settled her into a chair when Redding appeared in front of us.

Satisfaction blossomed in my chest at the red, angry flush suffusing his face.

Charlotte, seeming to sense the tension gathering around her, glanced at the man. "Good evening, Warren."

"Redding, correct?" With one hand on Abby's shoulder, anchoring her, I reached the other across the table toward Redding.

He ignored the gesture, his mouth tight, expression ugly—a bulldog ready to fight.

"You don't want to cause a scene, now do you?" I murmured and pointedly glanced at my hand. I was in control here, and he needed to realize that up front.

The man reached out a thick paw and grasped mine. A crushing grip. I stared into his eyes and let him see exactly how little he could hurt me. Then returned the favor.

His wince was barely perceptible, but it brought a smile to my face. "It's a pleasure to meet one of my father's oldest friends," I finally said.

Redding extricated his hand from my grip. "Let's not play games, Agozi."

I glanced around the room. Charlotte stood just on the other side of Abby, silent, dark eyes watchful, her hand on a seat back. The chairs immediately on either side of us were empty, but not for long. There were already eyes watching our exchange with interest, just as Abby's friend was.

"Society is a game, isn't it?" I said. A front to cover up who you really were. Not that different from the life I'd lived, I suddenly realized. "Reality doesn't surface till the masks come off."

"Why are you here?" he asked.

"Why do you think?" I tilted my head, let my gaze wander down his tight tux and back up. Taking his measure. Finding him wanting. "It's recently come to my attention that my father's estate is in the wrong hands. I'll be taking it back." I scanned the room glittering with wealth and power. "And everything that goes with it."

Redding's eyes narrowed. "You've been gone a long time, son. Walking back in, picking up where your father and uncle left off—that's not going to be as easy as you think."

Son. That one word was like a struck match, sending my anger into a bonfire of rage. I leaned across the table, getting close. Keeping the words just between us. "I think you're the one who needs to be careful, Redding. You think that army you've hired can keep you safe? You have no idea who you're dealing with."

Redding's gaze dropped to Abby, trembling beneath my hand. "I know exactly who I'm dealing with." His dark eyes speared me. "A man like you can't afford to have weaknesses, can he?" He arched the brow. "Think about that very carefully, Agozi. I'll be in touch."

With a sketchy bow in Abby's direction, Redding turned to stride from the ballroom.

"Levi?"

Charlotte's voice was uncertain. When I glanced her way, her hand was on Abby's shoulder. Supporting her. Ready to have her back. That one small gesture warmed me to her in a way nothing else could.

"It's all right," I assured her. And Abby. "Nothing to worry about tonight."

The couple next to me arrived to take their seats. I sat as well, took Abby's hand in my lap, letting my heat against her side steady her. But all the while, my gaze was on the door to the ballroom, the last place I had seen my enemy. The last glimpse I'd had of the man who wanted to destroy me and everyone around me. I knew it now, right down to the foundation of my soul—Redding was the one. He'd started this.

And he planned to finish it, no matter what obstacles I threw in his way.

Chapter Nineteen

Abby dug her fork tines into a dry triangle of chocolate cake while the series of ass-kissing speeches went on. I'd lost track of who was talking a half hour ago following the speech where Sister Margaret honored several of the St. Mary's residents who had achieved remarkable goals after being, literally, at rock bottom. Graduating from college. Starting their own business. Buying a house for their small children. Abby had watched, tears in her eyes, and I knew the stories reminded her of her mother and all that she'd achieved. And all she'd ultimately lost.

Now I eased forward until my chest cushioned Abby's back where she sat sideways in her chair, and tugged her fork away from its owner-inflicted cake massacre. My tongue had protested halfway through the rubbery chicken, so my cake sat untouched in the middle of the table. I dipped my head until my lips barely brushed Abby's shoulder. "I think it's dead; no need to torture the poor thing," I murmured.

She turned just enough to rub our cheeks together. "You would know. I'll defer to your expertise."

I managed to keep my snort between us. "Right. This expert says we should pick up some edible dinner on the way home. How could this possibly be ten-thousand-a-plate food?"

"It doesn't matter how much you pay, the food is always the same."

She'd had enough experience with these events to know. Thank fuck we managed to escape not long after the speeches finally petered out. It was late, but I made a call and, minutes later, swung by Miguel's. When I returned to the car, I was carrying two large sacks of steaming hot, fragrant Mexican food.

Abby stared at the bags liked I'd scavenged pots of gold. "How did you manage that?" she asked, eyeing the closed sign prominently displayed on the door.

I focused on the road. "Miguel and I go way back." Even farther than she and Charlotte did.

I didn't tell her we'd run the streets together as teens. When Miguel ended up on the wrong side of a gang after sleeping with their leader's sister, I'd taken care of the situation. When you wake up from a sound sleep with a knife against your balls, you'll promise anything—and Mr. Tough Guy had.

Now when I dropped by, Miguel refused to let me pay. I glanced at Abby, grinning at the anticipation lighting her eyes. "You'll never have better fajitas than this, I promise you."

Abby agreed with her first bite of the perfectly spiced steak as we sat around the table with my brothers back at the safe house, plates full of food in front of each of us.

"Better than the foie-whatever and champagne you had at the dinner?" Eli asked.

"God, yes," Abby moaned around a mouthful. "You can't imagine how many of those god-awful plates I've had through the years. This is better by miles."

When our bellies were full, we took our beers into the living room. Much as I'd rather focus on the soft weight of Abby curled against my side, I knew there was too much to discuss tonight. "What have you found, E?"

"You saw the whitewashed bio I sent, right?" he asked, referring to Redding, then shook his head, knowing the question was unnecessary. "I don't know a lot for certain—Hacr Tech deals in advanced technological concepts, including government research contracts, so information isn't easy to come by."

"Not yet," Remi pointed out. And he was right; give Eli enough time and he could hack anything, no matter how much security was involved.

Eli rolled his eyes, his *duh* silent but obvious. "Redding is CEO of Hacr. I'm assuming that's how he got involved with Chadwick; they'd have worked together once the trust went under Chadwick's control."

"So he's a scientist?" Abby asked.

"He's a politician. He's the decision maker at Hacr, so he'd have his finger in all the pies there."

"And Chadwick has majority control of the company shares because of the trust," Remi added. "Between the two of them, that's pretty much unbreakable control of the company."

"And a shit ton of money," Eli said. "Hacr has grown exponentially in the past twenty years since Redding was appointed."

"Are they working on anything that would warrant murder?" I asked.

"Oh yeah. Plenty." Eli crossed the room to a desk in the corner and riffled through some papers. "Over the years the teams at Hacr have garnered dozens of patents, published research in all the most prestigious journals—"

"Wouldn't Redding's position as CEO gain him a fortune of his own?" Abby asked.

"Of course." Apparently finding what he was looking for, Eli brought a stack of sheets to me. "I'll know more tomorrow about which projects are currently viable, but if rumor is right, this"—he pointed at the papers—"might be the reason Redding has gotten trigger-happy."

I glanced over the models and graphs with bleary eyes. "What is it?"

Eli humphed. I gave him a tired glare, Abby's yawn beside me punctuating my point.

Sitting on the coffee table, Eli picked up his beer. "It's a completely secure, completely unhackable system for super-sensitive communication."

"Bullshit." I flipped a couple of pages. "Nothing is completely hack-proof."

"This is. Or would be."

I set the papers on the table. "Give me the *Cliff Notes* version. Please."

"It's a concept called quantum entanglement communication."

From the looks on Abby's and Remi's faces, they didn't understand Eli's words any more than I did.

"The most basic explanation is that you have two photons that are created together, like twins. Two halves of a whole. What happens to one, happens to the other, no matter how far apart the photons are geographically."

"Like telepathic communication, except with particles?" Remi asked.

"I'd need to be a scientist to know how it works, douchebag."

Remi grunted.

"Anyway, you have a line of these particles in one location, and the photons' 'twins,' for lack of a better term, in a different location, in the exact same order. Like a computer, you can alter the particles so they each turn 'on' or 'off'—"

"Ones and zeros," I put in.

"Yeah, it reads as ones and zeros. When you turn one on or off, its twin responds too."

"And you can send a message without being in the same location or connecting the groups by wires or computers or anything else?"

Eli nodded. "Exactly. There's nothing to hack. You have to have the corresponding photons to read the message."

I still wasn't certain I understood it, but Eli seemed to, and that was all I needed. The implications, however…

"Every government in the world would be scrambling to acquire a system like that," Remi said.

Eli nodded. "And every criminal organization."

"They've actually done this?" I asked. "They're not just in the theoretical stages?"

"Unknown," Eli said. "The idea has been around in theory for decades. Their team of scientists has published several papers on the subject in the past few years, but recently there's been some rumors in the security community that Hacr is on the verge of a breakthrough."

"They'd basically be printing money," I said. No wonder this wasn't just about the trust. Nineteen years of investments and interest on my parents' already substantial fortune would set someone up for life, probably more than one someones. But this... Anyone in control of such a significant development could become the most important person in the world.

This wasn't just about money. It was about power. Control.

Christ.

Abby yawned again, shifting beside me, her breast pressing against my arm. When I glanced at the clock, I realized it was well past midnight. "We need to hit the sack." We weren't going to figure this all out tonight. It would have to wait till tomorrow.

Abby threw me a grateful glance as she stood and stretched. "I want out of this dress," she said.

Eli and Remi choked, their laughter reviving Abby's sass. She flipped them the bird.

Honestly, I knew how she felt. It was time for this straitjacket of an outfit to come off. And with the added benefit of watching Abby strip, I had zero compunction about leaving my brothers to clean up our dinner.

In the bedroom Abby flicked on the bedside lamp, the soft glow warm on her skin. "At least this place has a decent bed," she said, her smile small. She had a point. Safe houses weren't made for comfort, something she'd experienced more than once.

I ripped the dangling bow tie away from my collar and dropped it to the floor beside my tux jacket, wondering if I could get away with burning the damn thing. "If you're uncomfortable, princess," I teased, "let me know. I'll fix it for you."

I was only half joking.

"Riiight." Deep green silk slid down her body. She was left bare from the waist up, a nude lace garter belt gracing her hips, the long straps clipped to creamy thigh-high hose. Tired as I was, my cock stirred.

Abby noticed the look in my eyes and laughed. "Keep the beast locked up. I'm way too tired for any of that."

I held back a smile as I stalked toward her, Abby retreating until her back hit the wall. Her hand came up to land on my bare chest where my shirt gaped open, but not to push me away. No, she settled it above my heart, absorbing the thump of it beating.

"I love you, Levi," she said. Simply. Quietly.

I went weak in the knees. Only planting my fists into the wall as I leaned over her kept me upright. "I love you, too," I said against her mouth.

A sweet, tired kiss was her reply; then she pushed me away. "Go get ready for bed, sexy."

I was smiling like a fool as I turned toward the bathroom.

Thoughts of giving Abby a foot rub, easing the ache from those far-too-tempting heels she'd worn all evening, maybe extending the massage up her perfect legs to places far more intimate, filled my brain when I walked back into the bedroom—and found Abby fast asleep on top of the covers, one small hand tucked beneath her cheek.

I stopped to stare, to absorb the moment—a moment most men would take for granted, possibly even get angry over. My woman was too tired for sex; how "real life" was that? What would it be like to have Abby asleep in our bed, exhausted from a day of caring for a child? Or desperate for sleep after the restless nights that came with pregnancy?

Less than half a year ago, I couldn't have imagined the desperate longing that filled my chest in that moment. Couldn't imagine a life where a wife was possible, much less a child. And now…

Abby had asked how revealing my identity would affect my life, my brothers' lives. I still didn't know. Even with my parents' money, I couldn't imagine not working, not making the world more just, one kill at a time. But maybe—

A buzz caught my attention. At first I couldn't place it, staring around the room before I scrambled toward the tuxedo jacket I'd dropped on the floor with so little consideration. In the outer pocket, a slim phone, barely thicker than a credit card, waited, screen lit up. *Unknown Caller*, it said. I tapped to accept the call.

Silence on the other end.

"Who is this?" I demanded. Not *how did you get this phone in my jacket?* I'd settled it on the back of my chair during dinner. Opportunity—and my enemies had taken it.

I stared down at Abby, sound asleep, and barely held back a growl. "Who. Is this?"

"Agozi, I'm glad you found my little gift."

Fuck all. Redding.

Chapter Twenty

"He wants you to what?"

I glared Remi down. "Shut the fuck up. I don't want Abby hearing you."

"You're going to hide this from her?" Eli asked. "Not a good idea, bro."

Probably not, but it was the only way I could do what I had to. If, in the back of my mind, all I could focus on was her worrying, I'd be too divided to stay safe. Redding would have a foothold, and I couldn't allow him one.

"Just get everything ready," I snapped.

"And what about Abby?" Remi nodded at the phone in my hand. "I can guarantee he tracked that here. She's not safe."

"We'll get her out before we hit the meet up."

"Get her where?" Remi growled. "Because if you think you're walking into that mansion without both of us covering you, you're fucking insane."

I wasn't insane, nor was I stupid. "We'll take her to Mrs. Sanderson's. She'll be safe there for a couple of hours."

"Levi…" Remi shook his head like I definitely wasn't as bright as he'd thought. "If they know we're connected enough to throw Molotov cocktails through her windows, they know everything about her life. Including her visits to Geneva Sanderson."

"They set her house on fire because we were with her." I scrubbed a hand over my face, dug into my tired eyes. I had been up all night trying to figure out a plan. The only thing I knew was that a meeting with the enemy would happen one way or the other. It was better for it to happen when we could strategize ahead of time. "Besides, they'll be concentrating on the mansion. I'm a far bigger threat than Abby will ever be."

She was just collateral damage. Or would be if I didn't stop this fucker in his tracks. The mansion was practically a compound now with Rathlin's army there, and they wouldn't let me inside if I was armed. But meeting with Redding, discovering what his plan was, evaluating his defenses up close was worth the risk. My brothers stationed outside with sniper rifles would keep things even any day.

Remi waited a moment, weighing the odds just like I had. Just like I'd taught him to do. When his shoulders slumped, I knew he'd come to the same conclusion. He gave me a reluctant nod. "We'll get ready."

I jerked my chin in gratitude, not that I'd had any doubts. They would always have my back, even if there was no chance of winning.

When I turned to face the bedroom door, I sucked in a sharp, deep breath and pushed away the long night, the decisions, the killing instinct that had risen at the sound of Redding's voice invading the sanctity of my and Abby's most intimate space. The instinct that hadn't quite faded. I'd never gone into a fight worried I wouldn't come out alive, not since my brothers had gotten old enough to survive without my protection. That was one thing that made me so good at what I did—lack of fear. If you weren't afraid of dying, you wouldn't hesitate. But knowing Abby was waiting on the other side... Hell if it didn't make me worry. Not because she couldn't survive on her own; the problem was, I didn't want her to. Ever.

That fear was dangerous. It got you killed. I needed to be stone-cold when I walked into that mansion, the killer the only part of me that was aware. For the first time ever, I doubted I could do that.

The bed was empty when I entered, but the sound of the shower behind the closed bathroom door told me exactly where to go. I left a trail of clothes in my wake as I followed the call.

Steam shrouded the bathroom. Through the glass shower door, I savored the mottled view of her body stretched beneath the spray, hands sifting through the burgundy strands of her wet hair as soap slid from the mass to trace the graceful lines of her back, ass, legs. Fucking A, she made me hard. Hungry. I wasn't a sentimental man—before Abby, I would've argued that I had no emotions. But deep inside where no one could see, there was a lockbox full of memories just like this one. Moments that proved to me that life could still be good, could still be worth living. Worth fighting for.

The animal part of me raised its head, staring at its mate. Wanting to wade into battle soaked in her scent.

The man wanted the same.

"Are you going to stand there staring or come in here with me?" Abby asked. She was leaning close to the glass, her palm resting against it at just the right angle to obscure my view of her breast. A hint of a smile peeped at me through the mist.

Hunger clogged my throat. "I'm definitely coming in, little bird," I growled. *In more ways than one.*

The door to the shower clicked open.

Abby slid back in the narrow tub as I stepped inside and closed the door behind me. The spray hit the back of her head, and then she was beyond it, the trail of water as much of a barrier to my sight as the glass had been. Unacceptable. I reached up and pushed the showerhead to one side, removing the obstacle between me and what I wanted.

Abby's eyes darkened as they trailed along my raised bicep, the thick muscles of my chest. "You've been up awhile."

I glanced down at the tightening length between my thighs, then arched a brow. "Since the minute I heard you move."

She blushed. The pink wave moved from cheeks to neck to just above the smooth mounds of her breasts like it was directing my attention where it wanted me to go, and I was happy to comply. Moving in, I grasped Abby by her arms and dragged her around, switching our places, putting her back to my front. My cock went from tight to rock-hard as it slid along the crack of her ass.

Abby moaned. Her head tipped back to rest in the hollow under my collarbone, exposing the frantic beat of her heart in her throat. I couldn't resist. When my teeth gripped her skin and my tongue stroked with languid pleasure, she went to her tiptoes to give me more.

Fuck, the view down her body. A year and a half after our first night together, it still took me by surprise how beautiful she was. It shook me down to my marrow. I took advantage of the water coating her skin to slide my hands around her narrow waist, up her rib cage to cup the full weight of her breasts in my palms. A perfect fit.

Her breath hitched. So did mine.

Abby had mouthwatering strawberry-pink nipples that got tighter every time I touched them. Taking both between thumbs and forefingers, I rolled them delicately.

She whimpered.

I pinched.

"Levi!"

I was a dying man sucking back air, desperate to keep control. "Put your hands on the wall for me."

Abby tried to step forward, but I dropped a hand to her hip to keep her in place. "From here, little bird," I said, the words ragged.

She leaned forward slowly, bending from the waist to stretch out, back flat. Her palms hit the tile in front of her. The angle dragged her cream-coated slit along my cock, and when I dipped my hips, I slid right to her opening—and inside.

Abby squeaked. "Not quite…ready…"

My chuckle was strained. "Don't worry; I'll take care of that." Her grip on my cock was so tight I thought I would choke. Holding myself deep inside, I reached for her dangling breasts. Abby had the most sensitive breasts—a few minutes sucking them, playing with them, and she could come with a mere breath on her clit. I used that knowledge ruthlessly now, pinching and pulling, twisting, scraping my palms over the tight nubs, massaging the full globes. Abby panted and squirmed, her cream flooding my cock over and over until I thought I'd go insane if I had to hold still a moment longer.

But I waited, pressed as hard and deep as I could inside her, until with a sharp cry she spasmed around my erection.

Harsh breathing filled the tiny bathtub. "Oh God."

"You're not done," I warned her. I wasn't done. Not by a long shot.

She whined when I dropped to my knees, but a firm slap on one tender ass cheek kept her in place. A moan escaped—from her, from me—when my tongue speared inside her. I lapped up the cream that waited for me there, sought out every drop as deep as I could delve, savoring the tang of her pleasure in my mouth. I licked her folds, drew them in. Sucked gently until Abby was rocking back toward me, tipping her hips in a desperate attempt to get her clit between my lips.

It wasn't my lips that I gave her. When the edges of my teeth grabbed her sensitive nub, she gasped. My name echoed off the shower walls in a shrill cry when I shook my head, scraping her clit roughly.

Tearing myself away was like tearing out my heart, but I needed her face-to-face, needed to stare deep into her eyes as I fucked her as hard as I could. In seconds I had Abby out of the shower and lifted onto the long counter next to the sink. She spread her legs wide immediately, expression as desperate as if she'd never come, and I slammed myself deep inside with a hard, harsh groan.

"Abby, Abby, Abby…" I chanted her name to the rhythm of my hips, lost in the pleasure of her core gloving me, her cervix tapping the tip of my cock, the slapping of my balls against her. Abby reached for my ass, and her nails dug in deep, pulled me hard against her. No, forced me. Begging me to fill her. The hard tips of her breasts scrubbed my chest, and I ducked my head to draw one into my mouth, smashing her nipple between my tongue and palate and sucking with desperate hunger—

And just like that, she went off again, clutching and crying and squeezing my cock until a surge shot down my spine and I shot my load at the mouth of her womb, marking her as deeply as she'd marked me. So deep it touched my soul.

I'll be back for you, little bird. Nothing can keep me away. Nothing.

Chapter Twenty-One

The hurt in Abby's eyes when I left her at Mrs. Sanderson's tiny duplex haunted me as I drove out of town. I had refused to explain where we were going, just told her not to worry.

Eli was right. That plan had backfired big-time. But I'd have to deal with that when I returned.

Five miles out from the mansion, I pulled over to drop off Remi and Eli. They would hoof it the rest of the way, coming in from the east and west to set sniper positions we'd already selected—Eli at the tree house, Remi in a grove of trees on a rise opposite Eli's perch.

"They'll be expecting you," I warned them. Rathlin was no idiot.

"They'll be expecting something," Remi agreed. "Not us."

"They still haven't found the camera I planted," Eli said. "They won't be finding us."

"Just don't get cocky." I put extra bite into the command. The last time I brought them into danger, Remi had almost died. Since then I'd kept them well out of range. They weren't walking into the mansion with me, but Rathlin would step up patrols in the woods. I knew because it was exactly what I would do.

The humor dropped from Eli's face, and I saw my warrior side reflected in his light eyes. "We've got your back, Levi. Promise."

And we kept our promises. "You better."

"Let's go," Remi said and slammed the door shut.

I watched them jog into the nearby woods and disappear. An hour later I drove onto my parents' property. There were fifteen or twenty men waiting along the front drive, all fully armed. When I parked the car, it was Rathlin who came to my door.

"The mighty Assassin." His grin had an edge. "I never thought I'd see you face-to-face. Wish it was under better circumstances."

No, he didn't. I lifted my sunglasses, smirking when I saw his muscles go tight. A healthy caution was necessary in our business, even when you thought you had the upper hand. Rathlin was cocky, but he wasn't a dummy, just like I'd told my brothers. "Let's get this over with," I said, settling the glasses atop my head. I held out my arms.

Rathlin nodded at two of his men. They started the pat down at my boots, only hesitating when they reached the Kevlar vest covering my chest.

Rathlin raised a brow. "You know that has to come off."

"Fine." I turned to the still-open door of my car and moved to get in.

Rathlin held up a hand. "A vest isn't going to do you any good, man."

This time I was the one who raised a brow. "I know. You could aim for my head anytime. So why fight over the vest?"

He firmed his lips, obviously considering the argument—and maybe how badly his boss wanted me inside. "Fine. Loosen the straps and let my guys check under it."

He was thorough, I had to give him that. I left my keys in my car and followed him up the front steps when his men were finished. That was the only crack in my warrior cool, the moment I came face-to-face with that door. Remembering the last time we'd walked through it as a family, almost twenty years ago. And then I tucked the memory away, along with any emotion I dared to feel, and walked inside.

Rathlin made a beeline for the stairs. He hadn't even realized I'd stopped until one of his men called his name.

"Redding is upstairs," he said.

"I'm sure he is. Call him down."

Rathlin frowned. "Those aren't my orders."

"Gentlemen, tell your fearless leader why he shouldn't try to force me away from the wide-open first floor," I suggested.

A collective, somewhat smothered gasp echoed in the room as a tiny red dot appeared between Rathlin's eyes. He couldn't see it himself, but he didn't seem surprised when one of the goons who'd fondled my balls outside told him about it. I shook my head. "You know my reputation. What the fuck got you thinking I wouldn't know my enemy?" I jerked my chin toward the ceiling. "Call him down."

He did. I took the opportunity to walk toward the seating area in one corner of the large room, flanked by floor-to-ceiling windows. Rathlin frowned but didn't bother protesting.

Redding did. Obviously furious as he jogged down the stairs, he made his feelings even more plain with muttered curses as he crossed the living room. I didn't bother hiding my satisfaction.

Redding narrowed his eyes on me as Rathlin's men spread out, their backs to the windows like a living screen. I sincerely doubted that they were prepared to give their lives for Warren Redding, but I kept silent until the man stood in front of me.

"Didn't think we'd meet again so soon, did you?" the older man asked. "If you think you have any control over the situation, think again."

I let my gaze drift to the stairs and back. An ugly red flush crept up Redding's cheeks.

"One sniper doesn't give you the upper hand," Rathlin pointed out. He stood, legs spread, arms relaxed at his sides. He knew how this was going to play out, even if Redding didn't.

"No." I settled into a straight chair facing the couch and casually crossed one leg over the other. "It doesn't."

Immediately four red dots appeared, scattered across Redding's chest and face. The ring of men had no chance of covering every portion of the windows. And even if they had, well, I wasn't afraid to make a hole if I needed one.

"Now that we've compared dicks, have a seat." I waved a hand toward the couch like I owned the place, which technically I did.

"You don't realize it, but you're just like your uncle," Redding said tightly, taking a seat.

It wasn't a compliment, but if he thought I was as ruthless as Amos, I'd take it. "What do you want?"

Holding up a hand, Redding waited until a sheaf of papers was deposited in his palm, then shoved them across the coffee table in my direction. "I want you to sign these."

I didn't reach for them. "What do they say?"

"They sign over control of your shares in Hacr Tech to me."

"Cutting Chadwick out of the deal, huh?" It hadn't escaped my notice that the lawyer wasn't present.

"I have you to thank for that," Redding said. "I've been looking for a way to remove my partner for too many years. Now I can."

"And what do I get out of it?"

"You get to live," Redding said, pointing out the obvious.

I rolled my eyes.

"You and your family will be left in peace," he reiterated. "You may even keep the trust your parents so cleverly devised. With Hacr, I'll have no need of anyone else's money."

"Not with that top-secret communications system you're on the verge of releasing."

Redding actually looked impressed. "So you're more than a hired gun. Something of your father must live on then."

Not in me. I was who Amos Agozi had made me. My brothers had stood a fighting chance though; I'd sacrificed my own to be sure of it.

I considered the papers a moment, as if I would ever make a deal with this devil. "That's a very generous offer."

Redding grinned. "I thought so. Far more than what your uncle wanted to give you."

My muscles tried to tense, but I forced the reaction back. I couldn't afford to give Redding an inch. "My uncle?"

"Of course. You didn't think he came up with the idea on his own, did you? He wasn't happy to discover we had evidence of his participation in your parents' murders, nor that we were willing to use it against him after already using him to kill them in the first place." His smile went almost dreamy, as if a pleasant memory was coming back to him. "We had Amos by the balls back then—or he had us. It was a mutual vise, I'm sure, at least until his murder."

Redding narrowed his eyes. "That was you, wasn't it?" His gaze trailed over me, taking in the sight of a killer. "It was such a big mystery then, but I can see it now. Thank you."

"I didn't do it for you," I bit out. "I did it for them. Remember that." He'd just confessed to being an accessory to my parents' murders. Did he honestly believe I'd let him live?

"I really don't think there's anything you can do about it, is there?" he asked, glancing at the packed room.

"Not right this moment." We had each other by the balls, as he'd put it earlier, but it wouldn't stay that way.

"I don't kill unless it's necessary," Redding said. "With this agreement, it won't be necessary."

I snorted at that bit of bullshit. "You don't kill at all. You hire henchmen to do your dirty work and hope they'll keep you and your kingdom safe. News flash—you don't stand a chance against me."

"We'll see." He heaved a deep sigh. "Just sign the paperwork, son. All of this will go away. You can keep living your vigilante life guilt-free while squandering your parents' millions, if you so choose, and there will be zero threat against you and your brothers. If not for yourself, do it for them."

They wouldn't want that any more than I did. "Fuck you."

Redding stared me down a moment longer before slapping his thighs and standing. "Our business for today is concluded, then. Call your brothers off. You are free to go." He turned, hesitated. "Last chance, Agozi."

I didn't bother with an answer. We'd both known I was going to walk out of here from the get-go, and if he knew I was like Amos, then any hope he'd had that I would sign his agreement had been pure delusion. Let him have the final word if he wanted it.

It was the last concession I'd make, because I fully planned on having the last shot.

Chapter Twenty-Two

Remi and Eli met me at the drop point, and I took them to our new safe house before I went to get Abby. Ironically it was the same house Abby had run away from after I kidnapped her. I just hoped she didn't try it again given her mood when I'd dropped her off. Mrs. Sanderson always had a soothing effect on her; maybe I'd get lucky.

It took me approximately ten seconds before I realized there would be no getting lucky this time.

Abby stood on the little front patio, her arms crossed over her chest like she needed to hold herself together. I wanted to take her in my arms and do the job for her, but the anger in her eyes shouted for me to stay away.

"Answer me, Levi. Where did you go?"

I glanced at Mrs. Sanderson with what I hoped were pleading eyes, but the old woman merely shook her head. Her message was clear: *you're on your own, kid.*

Hiding my grimace, I admitted, "I had a meeting with Redding."

Abby choked. At least I'm pretty sure that's why her face was turning that awful shade of red, but maybe the death glare had something to do with it too.

"And you didn't tell me?"

Obviously. I was just as hyped on adrenaline and the aftermath of the confrontation as Abby was on anger, but another glance at Mrs. Sanderson convinced me not to verbalize that. I took a minute to clear the sarcasm from my voice.

"Abby, I know you want to be a part of everything, but you are not always going to know what I'm doing. That's the nature of my work, and a safety measure for you. It's just the way it is. The sooner you try to understand that, the less stress there will be for you." I dared a half step forward but didn't touch her, not like I wanted to. "You'll get used to it."

"I'll never get used to having you in danger."

And I guess I could understand that on some level. Military spouses, I was sure, never stopped worrying. Cops, Feds—some occupations wouldn't allow you not to worry. But what I did was dangerous; there was no way to stop that.

"Abby—"

She threw a hand up. "Not now." And shoved past me.

I turned to watch her walk toward the SUV, and wished I was someone else, somehow who came without all the complications that this life had wrapped me in. But I wasn't.

You knew that going in. Don't let one setback stop you. Make it work.

"She does get it, you know."

I faced Mrs. Sanderson. Abby called her Geneva, but I couldn't bring myself to do that. I respected her too much. Her kind brown eyes had faded some in the couple of years I'd known her, but they were still full of wisdom. "Does she?"

The older woman reached a wizened hand to grab my wrist. Touching was something I had never allowed before Abby came into my life. I'd gone years without any more personal a touch than a quick screw in a back alley. My wild redhead had taught me the value of physical connection, and somehow over the past few months, that connection had extended to Geneva Sanderson. She had become like a grandmother to Abby and, by association, to me. At least what I imagined a grandmother would be like.

A smile deepened the wrinkles on each side of her mouth. "She does. She just has no way to get out her worry. Fear always sharpens the tongue."

I glanced down at my wrist and laid my palm over hers. No words came to mind, but Mrs. Sanderson didn't need any. She just held tight and let me absorb her understanding.

Finally I stepped back. "Thank you."

"Bring her back soon, honey. That's thanks enough," she said, passing me Abby's coat.

I brushed a kiss along her cheek and turned to go. I could barely see the edge of Abby's red hair around the headrest, the color glinting in the sun passing through the windshield, and something about the vibrant color settled the emotion clogging my chest as I crossed the lawn. We needed to get back to the safe house, talk, work things out. Hell, if she needed to yell at me, I'd let her. Whatever it took, I'd—

Between one step and the next, my world exploded around me.

Hitting the ground flat on my back drove every bit of air from my lungs. I gasped, choked. Where was Mrs. Sanderson? She'd been behind me, near the front door. What—

I couldn't hear anything. It was like I'd been stuffed into a balloon, echoing with my heaving breath and the thoughts in my head, but no sound.

Nothing. And my skin. It cringed away from what I finally realized was a fireball of silent heat directly in front of me, searing me, cooking me in my clothes.

It was only then that the pieces came together.

The blast.

The car.

Abby.

"Abby!" Her name was ripped from my lungs, faint in my ears. I screamed it again as I rolled to my side, fighting my bruised and uncooperative body to get up, get to her. Harsh flames blocked my view, but I crawled, then stumbled to the other side of the inferno, only to find it fully consumed. That didn't stop me. Lost in the numb silence that had taken over my world, I had only one thought: Get to Abby.

Get her out.

Get her out, goddamn it!

I was reaching for the passenger-side door when rough hands jerked me back. Even with my skin blistering, I fought them, desperate to get inside. More hands joined the first, ripping at me, forcing me away from the car. They were yelling, I could hear that, but nothing registered. Nothing but the heat and the flames and the agony. Not until two words finally, finally penetrated the fog.

"She's gone!"

The fight went out of me. Rough hands dragged me back to a safe distance, and I let them, because all I could see, all I could comprehend was the roaring fire that consumed the small body in the front seat. My Abby.

Gone.

A roar came from out of nowhere, breaking the silence in my head, shattering the barrier that protected me from reality. It was only when my lungs ran out of air and I was forced to inhale that I realized the man screaming was me. That agony was me. That savage pain…me. They tried to get me up, tried to make me look away, but I fought them. And I watched. And I screamed.

Abby. Gone.

It was the faintest sound that broke through the chaos in my head. A cry. Not close, but… Someone hurt. Who?

Abby. Gone.

The cry came again, fragile, devastating. It needed to stop, to go away, leave me alone in the darkness and let me die. But it didn't. It rose again and again, a long, keening wail that I couldn't ignore. In increments so slow they were barely noticeable, I turned my head—and realized exactly who I was hearing.

Geneva Sanderson.

Her fragile body was crumpled on the lawn just past her front patio, a small bundle of cotton and bones that rocked back and forth as she cried out her grief. I stared at her, uncomprehending, wondering why Abby didn't come hold her, take care of her. Why she left the woman she loved like a mother alone.

When I looked back at the car, the dying funeral pyre, I knew.

Because Abby was gone.

Somehow I managed to get my feet under me, to get my body to cooperate. The sound of sirens barely registered as I stumbled across the yard. My skin felt too small for my body; my lungs hurt. My desert-dry eyes refused to tear despite the gut-wrenching need to cry. None of it mattered.

All that mattered was reaching the woman on the ground, and when I did, I dropped down beside her like my bones had turned to water, put my arms around her shaking shoulders, and pulled her tearstained face to my chest. And let her cry for both of us.

I have no idea how long we sat there. The fire department came, pushing back the crowds, and put out the fire. A thick blanket of some sort was draped over the area where the windshield would be, protecting the victim from prying eyes.

The victim. Abby. My Abby.

The police came, asked questions. I have no idea what I told them. I didn't care. Maybe they knew that, because they finally left us alone.

Neighbors came and took Mrs. Sanderson inside.

And still I sat and stared at the charred remains of my car. Holding vigil for the woman I loved more than my own life.

"Sir?"

I blinked.

"Sir?" A dark form crouched in front of me—the cop I'd spoken to earlier. His kind eyes and careful voice made me want to punch his pristine teeth out. "Sir, is there someone I should call for you?"

"Call?" I choked out. The word clicked in my brain. My brothers. I needed to call my brothers, but I couldn't even fathom saying the words I'd need to say out loud. Abby was gone. How did I tell them I had failed to protect the most important person in my life? How?

"Sir, do you have a cell phone?"

I found myself fishing in my pocket, pulling out my phone. The screen lit up, and by rote I entered the security code with blackened, blistered fingers. The home screen was so bright it burned my aching retinas.

"Let me help you." The cop reached for the cell, but before he could grasp it, an incoming text pinged.

The message preview flashed on the screen for no more than a couple of seconds, but what I saw will forever be burned in my memory. One little sentence that smashed the rubble that was all that was left of my world. One sentence, that was all it took.

You had your chance to stop this.

Nothing more. Nothing else was needed. I squeezed the case in my hand, imagining Redding's neck, imagining that the moment the plastic crumpled into pieces, I was crushing his spine. The cop watched in confusion as I dropped the phone to the ground and stomped it, pulverized every last piece until all that was left was a pile of plastic shards and metal. My fingers dripped blood from various cuts and broken blisters, but I didn't register the pain. The agony inside was all I could handle. Nothing more.

Not until I really did have my hands around Warren Redding's throat. Repentance might be good for the soul, but not Redding's. He would die with his sins, and if I had my way, I'd follow him to the depths of hell and kill him all over again.

Abby was gone. Nothing would bring her back. And as I sat on the grass, numb to all but my rage, and watched the crowds disappear, the officials go back to their vehicles—watched the world slowly try to return to normal—I knew without a doubt that I didn't want to live without her. Not even my brothers could make me stay.

Redding would die, and then, God help me, so would I.

Chapter Twenty-Three

I'm not sure how he knew, but Detective Bryant arrived on the scene at some point. One minute I was pounding my phone into the ground, and the next, his weary eyes were right in front of me. He's the one that got me to my feet. He's the one that called my brothers. He's the one who forced me inside Mrs. Sanderson's duplex when officials arrived to remove the body.

The body. That's how they referred to her. As if she were just a thing, not the very breath in my lungs.

Mrs. Sanderson had sequestered herself in her bedroom, away from friends and family. Away from me. Which was as it should be. I was the monster who'd brought this horror into her life. Into Abby's life. And yet I found myself outside her door, palm and forehead laid against it, trying to soak up the love and energy and joy Abby had radiated around the older woman, as if she was still here. As if she wasn't...

I couldn't say *dead*. She was simply gone, but we would only be apart for a little while. I had to believe that. It was the only way to bear the pain long enough to do what had to be done.

"Come in here, honey," Mrs. Sanderson called through the door. She always called me *honey*, but this time it didn't make me laugh. I didn't question how she knew it was me either. She just did, and I opened the door like it was the gateway to the only hope I would ever have.

And closed it behind me. This was private. No one else should see.

Mrs. Sanderson's huddled frame was shrouded in an afghan where she sat in an old wooden rocking chair. All of her was still but her fingers, which plucked restlessly at the threads of the blanket. Bloodshot eyes rose to meet mine. She reached for me. "Come here."

So I came. I knelt at the old woman's feet and laid my palms in her lap. She covered them with her own.

"Mrs. Sanderson—"

"No more of that," she said sharply, but tears brought a glossy sheen to her brown eyes. "My girl is gone. Who else is going to call me Geneva like she did, like she was my own granddaughter?" She nodded slowly as if considering. "You will. Just like you're my own as well."

I squeezed my eyes shut at the grief in her voice and, to my horror, felt a single drop of moisture dripping down the side of my nose. A tear. I couldn't cry, couldn't give in. It would make me soft when I needed to be hard. Needed to be sharp.

But I opened my eyes to find the slightest smile on Geneva's lips, the barest tilting of the corners. The expression wasn't happy, more like…approval. "That's right, my boy. It hurts something powerful, and we all need time to grieve."

My grief was best spent behind a weapon, but I couldn't tell her that. Instead I followed the urging of her hand at the back of my head and rested a cheek on her knee. There I absorbed the generosity of a woman who barely knew me, and felt my rage grow as I soaked up her pain.

A faint knock came at the door. "Levi, your brothers are here."

My gut went tight. I glanced up at Geneva. "I have to go."

She patted my cheek. Not in that condescending way some old people use; no, I'd seen her pat Abby the same way, a gentle brushing that somehow signaled care and understanding all in one touch. I even found myself leaning into her fingers as if I could siphon off some of her strength, when really I should be the one who was strong.

Not gonna happen. Not tonight. I'd save my strength for facing Redding.

"Go on then," Geneva said finally. "I'm sure your brothers need you. I'll be here."

I watched her gaze drift to the window next to her, to the small garden Abby had helped her plant behind the duplex last spring. She sighed. "Let me know…"

There was so much to know: arrangements for Abby, what the police might find out, who was behind this. That last bit of information would most likely shatter any relationship between Geneva and me, but I'd share it. Not right now, but when the time was right.

For now I had a man to destroy.

"I will," I said, letting everything else fall away. I stood and leaned over her, feeling the familiar papery texture of her cheek as I kissed her. "You rest."

She nodded, but I could see in her eyes that she wouldn't rest anytime soon. The moment we'd lost the best thing in our worlds would be on constant repeat in our brains until we died.

I closed the bedroom door behind me and was in the living room with barely two steps down the tiny hall. Not long enough to get my shit together, but it would have to do. Remi and Eli stood near the front door with Bryant, the three big men seeming to take up the whole room. I nodded to the small group of strangers opposite them and ushered my brothers and Bryant out the door.

"Levi, God—"

I didn't know who spoke; it didn't matter. I held up my hand, took a moment to force composure into my voice. "Not right now. I can't…" I shook my head, grateful as all fuck that aside from yards of damaged pavement and strings of yellow police tape, the evidence of what had happened mere hours ago was gone. "I just can't right now."

When I glanced their way, I could read understanding in my brothers' eyes.

"This was Redding," I said.

Not surprisingly, no one argued. Just nods all around. Describing the text I'd received did elicit some harsh, if hushed, profanity. We weren't the only ones still outside.

"Where's the SIM card, Levi?" Bryant asked.

"Doesn't matter," I told him.

Frustration roughened Bryant's voice, as if he already knew he wasn't going to win. "Of course it does. You can't let this go unpunished. With that text as evidence, he will get all the punishment he deserves."

"Oh, he'll be punished," Remi said. "He'll know hell before he's through."

Bryant rubbed a hand over his face. "You can't go after him. Let me bring him in. Let me do this right."

With Redding's money? He'd never see the inside of a jail cell, evidence or not.

"Who said we were going after him?" Eli asked.

Because that would've been stupid. Bryant was a good guy, but no way would he be on board for vigilante justice. Which was why he didn't need to know about it.

Afterward he could come after us if he wanted to. I'd make sure my brothers were safe before…

I glanced at the blackened pavement nearby and felt bile rise to the back of my throat. "I need to get out of here."

"Levi."

I hit Bryant like a freight train, my fists tangled in either side of his collar, my face right up in his. "I need. To go."

Bryant raised his hands out to his sides. "Okay, got it." He straightened as I released him, and tired sympathy settled over his face. "Just…be careful. And if you change your mind—" He paused, then shook his head. "Just call me."

I walked away without another word. I appreciated the man—which surprised me, him being a cop and me being what I was—but I couldn't let him interfere. We never harmed the innocent, that was a rule, but Redding and Chadwick weren't innocent, and they wouldn't go down if we left this up to someone else. They'd gotten away with too much already. No, this was our job.

And I was looking forward to it.

Remi and Eli flanked me as we crossed to their SUV, parked a block away. The thought of climbing inside made my skin shrivel, but after a thorough check, we did it anyway. Remi started the car.

We drove for five minutes without a word. I finally broke the silence.

"Contact Luka Sokolov."

Remi jerked as if he'd been deep in thought. That name certainly broke him out of it. Once a major player in our world, Sokolov had gone legit several years ago. Now he was the best security expert money could buy.

"Why?"

"I want his best and brightest," I said. "Whatever the price. They'll be staying with Geneva until this is over. Make sure," I bit out, "that they're worthy of her respect. She's to be protected at all costs and treated as an innocent. Got it?"

Meaning they'd take better care of her than a nanny would, only with the added benefit of plenty of firepower. Sokolov ran a clean operation, or as clean an operation as he could considering the things he dealt with. Cleaner than mine. I shouldn't trust Geneva to anyone but the best—me and my brothers—but since I had to be elsewhere, this was as close to the best as I could get.

"What else?" Eli asked.

"What have you seen on the surveillance footage since I left the mansion?"

Eli leaned forward, his head between my seat and Remi's. "Redding made a hasty retreat. He left a skeleton crew behind, but I don't know where he's going or why."

I knew the why. He'd already planned the hit, and he knew I could get into the mansion if I needed to. "He's gone somewhere with more security. Find it."

"Will do, bro."

"We need to talk about Abby," Remi said quietly.

No, we didn't. I turned my head to stare out the window, ignoring his words.

"She was our family too, you know," he said stubbornly.

She was. *Is.* Even death couldn't destroy that. "I know."

"We'll take care of her," Remi promised. "Whatever she needs, we'll take care of it as soon as they release her."

He meant a burial. For the woman I loved. I couldn't bring myself to tell him he'd be burying me too. "Okay." I stuffed down my emotions like garbage in an overflowing trash can and cleared my throat. "Take us to the bunker."

The bunker wasn't so much a safe house as it was a weapons repository. We kept supplies there, restocking various hideaways as needed but keeping the bulk of our arsenal in a location we didn't frequent more than necessary, completely off the grid. The bunker had exactly what we needed right now.

No, not what *I* needed. What I needed was Abby in my arms, in my bed. In my life. If I couldn't have that, I'd settle for a war.

Chapter Twenty-Four

We loaded up what we thought we'd need from the bunker and went back to the safe house. Between turns cleaning up and eating, we researched where Redding might've gone. I had just wandered into the living room, still running a towel over my wet hair, when Eli called me to him.

"Check it out, bro."

On his screen was what looked like security camera footage. I leaned over the computer and squinted. "Location?"

"Hacr Technologies."

Eli had been researching the company since we'd found out about it, exploring the ins and outs, poking holes in the top-notch security. Apparently he'd cracked their camera system. On-screen, a guard post at the front of the complex stood to one side. A black SUV was stopped at the entry—

And guess who sat in the driver's seat.

Eli pointed to the lowered window on the vehicle. "There's Rathlin."

"When was this?"

"A couple hours after your meet and greet at the mansion." He fast-forwarded the footage, revealing a small caravan of SUVs, all with the windows tinted too dark to see inside, but my gut told me Redding was in one of them. And my gut had plenty of experience in situations like this.

Remi watched from over Eli's other shoulder. "Our rat ran to the most secure place he could find, didn't he?"

"Yep." Eli threw a grim smile at Remi. "Looks like we'll get that tour of Hacr sooner rather than later."

"The security at Hacr is top-notch," I pointed out. Most teams couldn't get past it, not without a world-class hacker on their side, which was probably what Redding was counting on. I leveled a stare on Eli.

"Dude, seriously." He shook his head, reached for his mouse, and proceeded to click through screen after screen of data, codes, camera footage. "I got this."

I smiled. The reflection I caught in my brother's eye looked more predator than pleased.

"I knew you'd come in handy sometime," Remi joked.

"Damn straight." Eli bumped fists with him.

By morning we had a workable plan, but I decided to hold off for what little cover darkness could provide us. We hit the sack, but when I closed my eyes, all I could see on the backs of my eyelids was the replay of the fireball that had consumed my world mere hours ago. I couldn't rest but instead lay for hours, the swoosh of my heart louder in my ears with every passing moment.

Bit by bit I replaced the memory of losing Abby with a movie of our plan, going over every step so often I knew each action would be automatic, no hesitation. My revenge played out on the screen of my mind, and it always ended the same way: Redding dead. Chadwick dead. Anyone who stood between me and them, dead.

I wouldn't stop until the movie became real life.

Two hours after dark we sat in a black van a mile from Hacr's front entrance.

"Go over it again," I told Eli.

He sighed like I was doubting his ability—I wasn't—but went over everything again. "Night staff is limited, and most security personnel is focused on the other buildings at night—where the good stuff is. We'll reduce the risk of legit personnel being hit if I take security off-line zone by zone."

"Buildings," I demanded.

"This one"—he pointed to the map in front of him, at a building near the front of the complex—"is the one we need. Mostly offices, conference rooms, supply areas. Mail. The rest of the buildings are labs and research facilities. This one's a garage," he said, pointing again. "Security and logistics here." Indicating the top floor of the executive office building where a small apartment had been built, he said, "Redding is likely here.

"The most important things in this building are the computers, and those are primarily monitored electronically and with alarms to protect against building intrusion."

"Redding wouldn't want his legitimate staff exposed to Rathlin's men," Remi said. "There's no way to pass them off as legitimate hires."

"Redding has pulled most of his legit security staff to other areas, leaving Rathlin's men with free rein in the executive building. Probably passing it off as extra protection for some kind of personal threat."

"He's not lying," Remi pointed out.

"No," I said, "but it won't help him." I nodded at Eli's screen. "How many bodies we looking at?"

He switched to a screen with red dots lit up over the blueprints of the building. "Maybe thirty, forty. Mostly on the top two floors. Scattered otherwise."

I grunted. "All right. You have the security zones timed to cut out?"

Eli tapped a couple of buttons, and a green bar highlighting the word *Activated* flashed across the middle of the screen. "Yep." He closed the lid on his laptop, keyed in a code on a small panel strapped to his wrist, and a miniature version of his screen appeared. "Ready. Let's lock and load."

Five minutes later we were headed toward the backside of the compound. It took less than thirty seconds to get the three of us through the fence.

"Thank God there are no dogs," Remi muttered as we loped through the trees toward the cleared area around the buildings.

"Right. Wouldn't want to see that lily-white ass of yours again." Eli chuckled. So did I, remembering the time as teens when a literal junkyard dog had caught the seat of Remi's pants as he jumped a fence.

Remi flipped us a bird.

Our quiet laughter died down when we reach the clearing. "Eli?" I asked.

Quiet tapping told me he was at work on the next phase of our plan.

"Go."

Even with the cameras on this side of the compound running recorded footage of the last five minutes, we kept low and quiet as we rushed toward the back entrance of the building we needed. Though we were already on the property, this sprint was like heading for the starting line. Once we hit that door, the fight was truly on. We would encounter resistance, we knew it, but I wasn't worried for me. My brothers might know what was at stake, even be willing to risk it, but I'd do everything in my power to keep them safe.

We reached the door.

The plan was to incapacitate as many men on the bottom three floors as we could, lessening the risk of being flanked later on, when we least expected it. We started in the basement locker rooms. At the first door I gestured Eli forward, let him do his magic on the electronic keypad. When the door clicked open, I took the left and Remi and Eli took the right.

Hugging the wall, I crept along the farthest row of lockers. Ahead, steam billowed out of the shower area. Slick skin could be hard to get a grip on, but I didn't need to—I'd brought dart guns. The ketamine injections would hurt, but only for a few seconds. Then it was nighty-night time.

I approached the door.

The sound of a locker door slamming—or maybe a head slamming into a locker door—reached me from the other side of the room, but I ignored it. If there was trouble, my brothers would signal me. As it was, I counted that side of the room taken care of. Instead I focused ahead, where two men shouted to each other over their shower stalls, debating the best locally brewed beer. I shot each man in the neck before they could decide—and didn't worry about catching them as they fell.

Back in the main room, Remi and Eli met me at the door. "All set?" I asked.

Eli gave me a thumbs-up.

We repeated the routine in the remaining basement rooms. The first floor was mostly empty at this time of night, though the front security guard put up a little fight before the ketamine kicked in. Remi dragged him behind his desk, and we proceeded to the second floor. Same procedure, same results, with only a handful of personnel. The third floor wouldn't be as easy.

"How's it looking?" I asked Eli as we crouched in the stairwell on the second floor.

Eli shrugged. "Same as before. Maybe fifteen goons on the next level."

Remi pulled a flash grenade from his belt. "Shock and awe, bro. Ready?"

Before we could start up the stairs, an upper level door opened. The three of us crouched behind the center half wall and waited, dart guns at the ready.

The door above clanked shut. Damn heavy steel doors. Laughter filtered down the stairwell, followed quickly by the *shtck* of a lighter and the faint scent of cigarette smoke.

I darted a glance around the wall. No one stood on the next level. They must still be back near the third-floor entry, directly over our heads. Probably relaxing against the wall for a break from prying eyes.

I motioned behind me for Remi and Eli to fade back and keep their eyes and ears open.

"What the fuck was Chadwick thinking?" A hushed snort echoed down the stairwell. I tilted my head, trying to decipher the situation with what clues I could gather.

"He wasn't thinking," Man Number Two said in a gravelly voice that spoke of a longtime smoking habit. "His dick was."

A pause, punctuated by the rustling of clothing and the occasional gusty exhale, came next.

"Like Redding is going to give up his prize to that idiot."

"Right?" Another exhale. "If he didn't give a shit, he'd let Rathlin take possession—and we'd be the ones with the prize."

"Too fucking bad too. I'd do some serious damage to get a piece of that."

I leaned back to glance at my brothers, a frown conveying my question: what the fuck were these men talking about? The trust? Why wouldn't Chadwick expect a piece of that?

Remi shook his head, looking equally puzzled. Eli shrugged.

Deciding it didn't matter, I turned back around and tensed, ready to storm up the stairs and tag them both with darts as quickly as possible.

"You think that's what Redding's after?" Man Number One asked. "I didn't peg him for the type."

"Every man's that type," the smoker said.

Feeling thoroughly confused, I leaned forward to place one booted foot as carefully as I could onto the first step up.

"I don't know. Redding is probably too old for his dick to work very often. And he's definitely not spry enough to avoid what that redhead's dishing out."

The faintest scratch of rubber against concrete came from behind me—too light for our friends to hear, but I glanced back sharply. Remi had eased a couple of steps closer, and as I looked, I realized his face had gone pasty white. One hand was up in a *wait* gesture.

I cocked a brow at him. His gaze darted up the stairs.

"More likely the chick's got money," the first man said. "Redding don't give a shit about kidnapping women for sex; he could have it anytime he wants to pay for it, and cheap too. No, it has something to do with money, I bet my ass on it."

The smoker grunted. "I'll take that bet. And maybe when he has what he wants—whatever that is—we'll get a turn."

The sound of shuffling—the men getting to their feet—echoed down the stairs, followed by a cigarette butt hitting the back wall above me. The upper door slammed shut, but I didn't move. I couldn't. My brain was too busy putting the pieces together, making five out of a two-plus-two equation I knew wasn't right. It couldn't be. And yet, when I glanced back at Remi and Eli, their faces reflected my confusion and, God help us, the smallest traces of hope. It was wrong, I knew it was wrong, but something inside me screamed that five was the right answer, no matter what my fucking head said.

"Remi?"

The word was barely a whisper, but there was fear there. Fear when I shouldn't be afraid. And then Remi nodded, his own eyes seeming to tear up as I stared into them and silently begged for reassurance. "Yeah," he said.

"Yeah," Eli said as well, coming up beside him. "Motherfucking yeah." He gripped my shoulder hard. "Did you hear that, Levi? Abby is alive!"

Chapter Twenty-Five

I felt like I'd been kicked in the head. Or maybe the heart. Abby was alive. Not dead, not blown into a million pieces by an inferno I had no possibility of stopping.

Alive.

My mind hit turbo speed in sixty seconds flat.

"She'll be with Redding." And apparently doing her own kind of damage, if what we'd overheard was true. I narrowed my eyes at Remi. "Plan B is in place, isn't it?"

He glared at me like that was the stupidest question he'd ever heard, but I ignored him. Right now I needed to think aloud, and he'd just have to deal. "Of course it is."

We needed to get as many of those men out of the third floor and out of our way as possible. Without Abby, we could take our time, comb the floor, take the men out one at a time. Not now. We were bypassing half our plan in favor of getting Abby to safety with all possible speed. "Come with me."

We retreated into the second-floor office space and holed up in the first room with a door we could close. "Ready?" I asked Remi.

He raised a detonator for the rest of us to see. "Am I ever not ready?"

The bomb he'd planted wasn't all that big. There would likely be minimal structural damage, but we'd placed it at the back of the first floor in the mail room, looking to get the most flammable material in one place as possible. A fire meant Rathlin's men couldn't ignore it; they had to deal, and that gave us time with them out of the way.

When Remi pressed the button, a muffled roar and hard shimmy reached us. Shouts in the stairwell barely traveled through the wall, and as I thought about all those men running for safety, concerned for their lives, my calm blew to bits just like the mail room had. The cool assassin was nowhere to be found right now, no matter how much I needed him. Rage was in control, all the anger that had boiled inside me at Abby's "death," the fury burning at the knowledge that Abby had been through a kidnapping, had suffered pain, fear, worry.

Fuck cool and emotionless—I had a flesh-and-blood target in my reach, and he'd pay for the hell he'd put me through. But he'd die for the hell he'd put Abby through.

By the time we sneaked back into the hallway, I'd channeled that rage into the hunt. Sticking to the outer edge of the staircase, we made our way silently up to the fourth floor. I caught sight of the guard stationed at the fourth-floor door mere seconds before he saw me, but that was all I needed to get a dart off. We could just as easily use regular weapons, but I'd rather not deal with the aftermath of thirty dead men and a clear motive attached to my now-public name. No, we'd stick to non-lethal—and reserve the *special* stuff for Redding and his cohort.

The guard dropped. Remi and I dragged him to one side while Eli set his position at the top of the stairs. "No one comes up," I told him, though he already knew. "No one. If you need to, drop more than just a flash bang." Eli had shut down the elevators before we came up, and in the enclosed stairwell, a flash bang might as well be an actual grenade going off. Any men attempting to reach the fourth floor via the stairs were about to have a very bad day.

He looped ear protection around his neck. "No worries. Go."

With Remi at my back, I approached the door. On the count of three, we rushed it.

We were at the back entry of the apartment, facing a long hallway. At the opposite end, a guard stood. I darted him before he could get his gun up. His cry brought another guard and Rathlin around the corner.

Remi took the second guard. Rathlin managed to retreat, leaving my second dart to hit the wall behind him instead of his arm, damn it. As I advanced, I could hear the guards from beyond the living area at the end of the hall rushing into the room. No female that I could detect. I didn't want Abby subjected to what I was about to do, but if it got her out of here… I prayed she was being kept in the bedroom.

With steady fingers I pulled the pin on a flash bang and tossed it around the corner into the crowd that was forming.

Even with my eyes closed, hands over my ears, and the protection of the wall, everything sheeted white. Sound died. I knew men must be stumbling around, disoriented, surprised, eardrums tortured, but I couldn't hear them. That didn't stop me or Remi from moving into the room. Amid the chaos, we darted three more guards.

Without conscious thought I took in the rest of the room. Abby and Redding were nowhere to be found. Rathlin had obviously used the couch for protection and now crouched behind it, at the farthest side of the room away from us, letting his men become cannon fodder. Chadwick, hands over his ears, ran for the executive office to the right of the living area. Remi followed, but I kept my attention on Rathlin.

He smirked at the dart gun in my right hand as he finally advanced. "Surely the big bad Levi didn't bring a dart gun to a gunfight." He had already pulled a GLOCK from the holster strapped to his thigh.

The man's voice sounded tinny in my ears. "Of course not." I waved my dart gun to get his attention, using the split second to pull a gun from behind my back. I might not be left-handed, but I could damn well shoot with either hand; I'd made sure of it. "I brought both."

"You won't need them."

Redding's voice came from my left, from the doorway to the bedroom contained in the apartment. Before I even looked, I knew what I was going to see, and I had to steel myself against it. I needed my eyes on Abby like I needed my next breath, needed to see that she was okay, that she was in one piece, but I couldn't let it overwhelm me, not now. No, the animal needed to hunt; the man would have to wait till later to care for his mate.

"Put the guns down," Redding said.

I looked; I had to. I took in the gun at Abby's temple, the mess of her hair, the tears in her eyes, the fierce determination that told me she'd fight till her last breath. The rough shape of her clothes and the bruises on her arms. And then I met Redding's triumphant gaze. "You're going to die, I promise you."

"I don't think so." He shoved the barrel harder against Abby's head, so hard it pushed her ear nearly to her shoulder. "Put them down. Now."

I eased toward the floor, carefully setting both guns on the carpet. Then stood.

"Kick them to me," Rathlin said.

I did.

He came toward me. I held Redding's gaze, not flinching, not wondering about Remi or Eli, even when a muffled roar and shouts came from the direction of the stairwell. I stared at Redding and I waited.

Rathlin had a long black zip tie in his hand now, presumably to cuff me. When he grabbed one arm, I stiffened it, using the resistance to swing my body around and come up behind him. The cry he gave as my fist connected with one of his kidneys said he'd be pissing blood for a day or two, but it didn't stop him. The fight was rough and dirty—and it hurt. I made sure to keep Rathlin between me and Redding, though the older man made no attempt to stop us. Probably thinking I didn't have a chance against his hired thug. When I dropped to the floor, swept Rathlin's feet out from under him, and punched him in the side of the head, knocking him out, I don't know who was more surprised, Rathlin or Redding.

I got to my feet, picking up Rathlin's gun on the way.

Redding scoffed, the sound not as steady as he'd probably like. "Go ahead, put a bullet in him. I don't care. He's as useless to me as that sniveling Chadwick."

I was pretty sure that sniveling Chadwick was currently tied up in the outer office. Remi would've stationed himself there to ensure no one rappelled up the elevator cables, giving me all the privacy I needed.

I took a step toward Redding. "I made you a promise." Another step. "Let her go and I might reconsider."

"She's my ticket out of here," Redding said, sidling in a wide arc around me toward the office door. "Besides, who will the police believe, a contract killer with a bloody past or an esteemed businessman who's put millions into his community?"

"Doesn't matter what they believe. You're not getting out of here alive."

He sneered, but I could see the sweat forming on his forehead. He continued to inch toward the door, and I continued to pivot, keeping him in my sights.

"With my money, I'll go somewhere no one can find me. And maybe I'll take your little prize here with me."

Remi chose that moment to step into the doorway Redding was headed for, gun at the ready. "I don't think so, motherfucker."

"Make your choice, Redding," I said.

He pointed the gun at me, his finger on the trigger. His hand was shaking. "I'll—"

Abby dropped her weight, bringing both arms up to break his hold. On the way down she bumped Redding so that he stumbled. Planting her foot on the inside of Redding's knee, she rode it all the way to the floor, putting her full weight on it. The sound of his knee disintegrating crackled through the air.

It was followed by a gunshot. A neat red hole appeared in the center of Redding's forehead, and his eyes went dead with his last breath.

I dropped Rathlin's gun and opened my arms for Abby.

In the middle of a job, closing your eyes is like writing your own death warrant; you just don't do it. But Abby's weight hitting me in the chest—I sucked in an actual fucking sob and closed my eyes and just…God… She was alive. She was alive and in my arms. I could vaguely hear Remi retreating back into the office, but I didn't care. I didn't look. Not with Abby against me again.

"Stop hugging your woman and let's get out of here," Remi said as he shoved Chadwick into the living room ahead of him. "Eli won't be holding them off much longer."

Chadwick stumbled, nearly losing his footing as his gaze landed on Redding. "What did you— What—" A ghastly white sheen took over his skin, everywhere but the swollen red nose that was covered in a bandage. Abby had good aim, as she'd already proven once tonight. "I—"

"This guy doesn't look so good," Remi said, pointing out the obvious.

"I couldn't give a shit," I said. I noticed Abby didn't look at the lawyer, just kept her face buried against me, and I wondered for the millionth time what had been done to her. "Set him up."

Chadwick's lawyerly physique was no match for Remi's strength. Forcing the man over to where Redding lay on the ground, he took the gun I passed him—Rathlin's gun—and pressed it into Chadwick's trembling hand.

"You can't— There'll be fingerprints. You'll—"

Remi leaned in. "Latex gloves. The only fingerprints will be yours and Rathlin's. We'll let the police sort out which of you is guilty."

"But…but…" Chadwick's words degenerated into meaningless rubble as Remi took aim at Redding's heart, his fingers over Chadwick's on the gun. When Remi "helped" him pull the trigger, Chadwick fainted.

"Made that easy," Remi said. He glanced at me and Abby, who still hadn't let go. I hadn't either. "We'll have to save the reunion, bro. Gotta split."

I rubbed a hand down Abby's back, then used it to urge her toward the stairwell. "Let's go, little bird."

"Okay."

The word was a blend of relief and gratitude. I knew exactly how she felt.

Abby followed Remi down the hall. He knocked twice on the stairwell door, paused, knocked twice again. A flash bang went off farther down the stairs, along with what sounded vaguely like a war cry, maybe a cowboy hollering—either way, it sounded like Eli was having fun. We waited for him to open the door.

"There you are, little sis," he said, jerking her into a hug. "Let's get you outta here."

With Remi bringing up the rear, Eli led our group up to the roof. We made quick work of setting up ropes. I sent everyone else down, but as I prepared to descend, I heard sirens coming from the front of the compound. "Eli?"

I glanced down and saw the panel on his wrist light up. While he assessed, I skimmed my way down the side of the building. Remi clicked a button after I landed, releasing the mechanisms on the roof that held the ropes in place, and he and I gathered the gear. Always take the evidence with you when you can.

"You'll never guess who's at the front gate," Eli said.

"Tell us on the run." I wrapped an arm around Abby and got her moving.

"Who?" Remi asked.

"Our boy Bryant," Eli said.

A muffled laugh escaped me, echoed by my brothers. "He's going to have an interesting night ahead of him, isn't he?"

"Better him than me," Remi said as he pulled the fence aside. He bowed from the waist. "After you, Abby."

She knelt in the grass, then stopped, staring up at us for a moment, and shook her head. "Thank you."

I leaned over, tipped her chin up, and grazed her mouth with mine. "Thank you, little bird. For being alive. Now go."

Chapter Twenty-Six

She's alive. She's alive. She's alive.

The refrain pounded in my head to the rhythm of my booted feet as we jogged toward the SUV. Abby ran in front of me, and I found myself analyzing her movement—was she as fluid as she should be, had she hesitated when she jumped that fallen limb? Were there injuries she hadn't told me about, that I couldn't see?

Of course there were wounds I couldn't see. She'd been held at gunpoint before—by her own father, no less—but that didn't mean the experience wouldn't leave scars.

Why the fuck couldn't I protect the most important person in my life?

But she's alive.

With the distraction at the front of the complex, we had no trouble escaping. At the SUV each of my brothers took a turn hugging Abby fiercely before shuffling her into the back seat. I pulled the latex gloves off my hands, passed them to Remi to dispose of along with his and Eli's, and followed after her, pulling her roughly into my lap.

"I knew you'd come," she whispered, burrowing against my chest. "I knew."

There'd been no way to know she was alive, but still I felt like shit for delaying even a day. The fact that she'd waited, worried, endured Lord knew what…

My mind raced as my hands roamed her body, searching for answers to questions I couldn't ask yet. Registering through touch that she was all right. Here. Real. I needed to feel every inch of her right fucking now.

Abby sat quietly in my arms, her beautiful eyes glittering up at me as if she knew exactly what I was doing and why.

"Bro, wait till we're home, yeah?" Eli chuckled, breaking the moment. "A little privacy is a great thing."

Remi punched him in the arm, hard. Eli winced, and in my lap, a little laugh escaped Abby.

"Asshole," I said, not without affection but with a heavy amount of exasperation.

Abby's laughter tickled my throat as she buried her face in the crook of my neck. Her weight on my legs, her arms around me, her face tucked against me drew a groan of relief from deep inside. I never thought I'd feel this again. Never thought I'd get a chance to fill my lungs with the scent of vanilla and flowers from her shampoo, absorb the warmth of her skin. My heart still felt ragged, torn apart, as if this wasn't real, but I had the evidence right here in my arms.

I buried my hands in her hair and lifted her head, needing to see her eyes, her light. "Holy fuck, Abby. I thought I'd lost you. I thought—"

Pain closed off my throat. Abby palmed my cheeks, her heat steadying me. "You couldn't lose me. I wouldn't let you."

"I watched the car blow up with you inside it," I said, my words more gravel than sound.

Abby's eyes widened. "You what?"

Remi steered the SUV onto the road, heading for home. "What did you think happened, Abby?"

"I… I don't know." She shook her head against my shoulder. "One minute I was about to get in the car. I was… I was angry."

I palmed her nape and squeezed. The anger didn't matter anymore; we'd both been taught that lesson.

"I wasn't really paying attention. I opened the door. Then there was something over my face"—she wiped a hand over her nose and mouth as a shudder shook her—"and…nothing. I don't remember anything after that, not till I woke up back there."

"You were at Hacr Technologies," Eli supplied.

Abby nodded, but I could tell that all she cared about was that she was no longer there.

"We'll call Bryant in the morning," I said above Abby's head. "He's the detective assigned to your case since it was tied to the fire at the house. I think he'll be happy to know you're alive."

Bryant also had his hands pretty full tonight. And while the detective probably had a very good idea what had happened back at Hacr, I didn't think he'd be pushing for too much more than the obvious explanations. Chadwick and Rathlin would take the fall for all of it now that Redding was dead. Odd though it seemed for someone like me to trust law enforcement, Bryant was a good man, and he had more than one reason to want Rathlin behind bars. His partner was still in the hospital, after all.

"Who the hell did they have in the car then?" Eli asked. I'd described to both of them that I'd seen Abby's hair from behind; it was the only thing that could have convinced me that she was the one in the passenger seat. Rathlin and Redding had really sold that move.

Abby shook her head. "I don't know."

Silence settled between us for a moment, filled with regret for the person who'd taken Abby's place. As glad as I was that she was here with me, I hated to see the innocent die. That wasn't the code we lived by.

"Are you okay?" I asked, unable to wait any longer. "Did they—"

Abby's head came up, her finger landing on my lips, cutting off the questions. "I'm okay. I promise." She stared fiercely into my eyes as if she knew where my nightmares led and was determined to obliterate them. "A few bruises, that's all." The slightest smirk tugged at her lips. "Chadwick had worse."

"We noticed," Remi crowed over his shoulder. "Good for you."

I didn't like it. She might say she was okay, but I wasn't sure which would give me more nightmares, reliving the explosion or imagining what had happened to her afterward. I pulled her tighter against me.

Abby clung right back.

She wasn't afraid, was she? "Nothing's gonna hurt you, little bird," I whispered in her ear. "I promise. Nothing."

Something warm and wet hit my neck. "I know."

But knowing and believing were two different things. My own mind kept tripping over the fact that she was alive despite her being in my arms. It was going to take a while for both of us to believe she was safe. Home.

When we got to the safe house, one glance at my brothers had them nodding toward me. A silent agreement—they'd take care of everything else; Abby was mine. I whisked her straight through the house to the master bedroom and into the adjoining bath. Abby immediately sank onto the closed toilet lid.

"I feel like I could sleep for a week," she said, "which makes no sense because I know I slept hard after they drugged me."

I tugged at the hem of her shirt. "I need you naked."

"Levi…"

I squatted in front of her, letting a hint of amusement sneak through, no matter how worried I was. "I need to see you, little bird. Feel you. Only then will I know you're truly home."

This wasn't about sex, though it certainly could be if Abby decided that's what she wanted. This was about absorbing her into me until I couldn't find where I ended and she began. Keeping her against me until the ragged pieces of my fucked-up soul came back together in some semblance of order. I could wait for the healing, but for now, I needed reality desperately.

Abby lifted her arms without argument. I undressed her almost as if she were a child—shirt off, shoes off, pants, underwear, everything. Her pale skin gleamed in the overhead light. The bruises, though, were black holes sucking the life out of me. "Abby."

"Hey." She pulled my chin up till I met her eyes. "I'm here. Bruises can heal. Exploding can't."

I knelt on the mat at her feet and brought my hands up to take the weight of her breasts. Not for sex, but because I needed the weight of her in my palms. I eased in close and let my lips brush hers. She opened to me, just like always.

And just like always, I slipped my tongue inside, delved deep, sucked and stroked and reveled in the feel of my woman. For the first time in forever, the raging animal of a killer inside me was silent. The thirst for blood, the addiction to the adrenaline high. What high could be better than the one I'd found with Abby? The one I'd thought I lost, only for it to be found again.

I scooped her into my arms. "I'm getting the stench of them off you, off us." I could still taste the ashy residue of the flash bangs we'd used, smell the aftermath of Redding's death on my clothes.

"Levi? Levi, look at me." Abby waited for me to look up. "I'm okay. I am. I can't imagine you thinking you'd watched me die." Her eyes took on a haunted glaze. "It doesn't matter how many times I have to say it, but I will until it finally sinks down deep, for good. *I am okay.*"

"I love you." The words were rocky and rough, but I meant them more than any words that had ever passed my tongue. "I love you. I can't live without you."

"I know." Abby dug her fingers into my hair. "I've got you. Don't worry." She brought our foreheads together. "I love you, Levi."

When I closed the shower door behind us, I closed out all the chaos—no more evil men, no brothers, no pasts, no danger and sorrow and agony too deep to be borne. In that small, warm, wet space, it was only Abby and me, and in the quiet beneath the water, I explored every inch of her, imprinting the feel of her on my mind and mouth and hands all over again, drowning myself in the joy of having her back. I showed her everything I knew about making her feel safe, and much later, when I finally lay beside her in the bed, spooned around her body, I knew I couldn't ask for more than to spend the rest of my life just like this.

With Abby. For fucking always.

Epilogue

One Month Later

Surreal. That was the only word to describe this moment. Standing at the double vanity in the bathroom that had once belonged to my parents, marble and chrome features gleaming. Abby brushing her teeth in her underwear. Me shaving the stubble off my face.

Surreal.

Abby rinsed her mouth, placed her toothbrush in the little caddy right next to mine—*surreal*—and turned to face me. "You're telling me you want a bat cave?"

A what? "You mean a man cave? No. I—"

"A bat cave. Like Batman. With his underground cavern of gadgets and deadly stealth car and all that."

The glint in her eye told me she was teasing. I rolled mine. "I'm no superhero, little bird."

She eased close, careful not to bump my arm as I scraped the razor over my cheek. "You are to me."

My chest got tight.

"Plus, you want a bat cave."

I rinsed the razor, then bent to cup water in my hands and splash it over my face just to cover the stupid grin I could feel trying to break free. I guess technically what I'd asked for as my thirtieth birthday present was pretty damn close—a "headquarters" in the basement of the mansion where my brothers and

I could work. Maybe we'd cover the walls in rock and order our own version of Batman's armored suit. In Kevlar, of course.

When I straightened, I snitched the towel from Abby's hand and dried my cheeks. Abby ran a thumb down the side of my jaw. "Missed a spot."

I had to kiss her then; she gave me no choice. Our lips met, parted, our tongues tangled, and heat surged through me, coalescing in my groin. The bite of my zipper as my cock hardened against it brought me back to reality far faster than I wanted it to.

I savored the taste of fresh mint and Abby on my tongue. "There," I whispered against her lips. "Did I get it that time?"

"You get it every time," she whispered back.

I rinsed the sink, and when I turned back to her, the mischief had left her eyes.

"You know, you don't have to work anymore," she said.

"Neither do you, but you're still going back to school." She hadn't given up her dream of becoming a nurse despite the distractions I'd thrown into her life the past few months. Or maybe because of them. With the three of us around, she needed an escape into a more *normal* reality. Knowing that didn't make me doubt our relationship anymore; it was what it was. We couldn't be without each other, so we made it work, however we needed to. And with the changes in my life, I needed her with me more than ever.

Abby bit her lip, shook her head. "Nursing is… It's not…"

"Dangerous?" I supplied. Because that was the difference. By nature, my job was deadly, sometimes to the people who did it, sometimes to the target.

"Being a nurse isn't guaranteed safety, you know." It was a factor in her life that I couldn't control, but I wouldn't take her dream from her.

Abby wanted me safe. Wanted to live our lives without fear. She was having to adjust to the reality of me as much as I was having to adjust to the reality of what I'd become since I'd turned thirty. Redding was dead and Chadwick was in jail for his murder, along with Rathlin as co-conspirator in Abby's abduction. Chadwick's partner, Manassas, had helped us straighten out the legal issues surrounding my trust and my parents' estate. As of five days ago on my birthday, the inheritance was completely mine, including the mansion. I was now majority shareholder in Hacr Technologies, and actively helping search for a new CEO. I had more money than I'd ever imagined—far more than I'd ever wanted—a lover I had every intention of making a permanent part of this life, and brothers who loved and needed me. It was all so normal.

So why did this normal man with a company to run and a fortune to oversee and a family to take care of need to take contracts as a hit man?

Because having a normal life didn't, in fact, make me normal at all. The killer still lived beneath the surface. He wasn't going away, and I had come to accept that.

"Being an assassin has a lot less of a guarantee than being a nurse," Abby was saying.

I hooked her around the waist and dragged her close. "Abby…"

"What?" she mumbled against my T-shirt. My nipple pebbled beneath her lips.

"You want to make the world a better place." A statement, not a question. Abby would save the world if she could. She'd already helped hundreds of women just like her mother through St. Mary's.

She nodded. That special Abby fragrance, vanilla and flowers, filled my nose. My cock perked up all over again.

"Me too," I said into her hair.

Her arms sneaked around me, up my back, to fist in my shirt on either side of my spine. Holding on tight. Not letting go. I squeezed my eyes shut.

I might not be a superhero, but eliminating the bad guys, protecting the innocent—I made the world a better place too. That part of me that others might hate, that killer instinct, served a purpose. And I couldn't give it up, not even for Abby.

What that meant for our future, how it played out in reality, I wasn't sure yet. I had Abby to guide me through the minefield of society and the obligations having such a huge fortune entailed. And I had a secret life no one but Abby and my brothers knew about.

Holy shit, I *was* Bruce Wayne.

I choked back a laugh. *Never tell Abby that. Ever.* And yet I couldn't keep a reluctant smile off my lips.

Abby raised her head, saw it, and kissed it away.

Long minutes later, she pulled back. "We need to get downstairs. Your brothers will be back with the food any minute."

I'd never really celebrated my birthday. My brothers had been too young to remember dates, and the memories of my parents had been too painful to acknowledge the milestones they should've been there to see. Abby refused to ignore it. Though we were running a week late after working to get the house ready and us moved in, she'd insisted we celebrate. When asked to choose my favorite meal, of course it had been Miguel's. Eli and Remi had gone to pick up our order.

The thought of Remi sent tension through my limbs. He'd been scarce since we'd resolved the whole Redding issue. I had a feeling I knew why—or rather, where he was disappearing to. But it wasn't up to me to confront him, not again. I'd had my head up my ass about Abby for a year and a half, after all. Watching her pull a baby-soft sweater over her lace bra and slide tight jeans up her perfect legs, I had to believe that Remi would get straight just like I had. I just hoped whoever the woman was, she was worth it.

"Go on down," I told Abby. "I'll be there in a minute." To celebrate my birthday.

Mind fucking blown.

After she headed downstairs, I crossed the massive master bedroom to the wall of windows at the opposite end. Though opaque from the outside looking in, the view from inside was achingly beautiful—the park-like backyard with its small patches of flowers scattered in strategic disarray; the thick forest that surrounded the house. If I strained, I could catch the glint of the creek curving through the trees.

All just as my parents had designed it. Their dream home, the place they'd chosen to raise three stair-step little boys.

I turned around, my stare taking in the master bedroom. The room my parents had died in. Redding had gutted it, turning it into an unrecognizable, over-the-top showcase. In the week before we'd moved in,

Abby had the rooms stripped and redone in classic lines and warm colors. Though not the same as I remembered growing up, it somehow felt familiar, comfortable. Like the home my parents had built for us in the few years we'd all been together.

I could feel them now. Call it a memory, call it ghosts; I didn't care. The warmth of their presence welcomed me, a balm I hadn't known I needed, healing the nightmares I'd never been able to escape. Until now.

I basked in that warmth until the sound of a car horn honking outside pulled me back to reality. Remi and Eli had returned. With a hard clearing of the knot in my throat, I went out the door and down the stairs. To my family. To celebrate.

We were home.

∞

Did you enjoy ASSASSIN'S PREY? If so, you can leave a review at your favorite retailer to tell other readers about the book. And thank you!

Want exciting extras from the ASSASSINS series? How about free book opportunities and bonus scenes? They're available only through my newsletter. **Sign up at www.ellasheridanauthor.com to get exclusive access!**

Before you go…

Things are just getting started for the Agozi brothers. Catch a glimpse of them in the SOUTHERN NIGHTS: ENIGMA novel, DENY ME.

And…

Remi wants what he believes he can't have. And maybe he's right. Find out in…

ASSASSIN'S HEART
Assassins 3

My brother believes he made me a killer. The truth is, I've always been different. I can smile while sliding a knife between your ribs—and not feel a moment of regret.

Until Leah.

A man like me shouldn't have a family. But the minute I opened my eyes from a coma and saw her, I knew I'd forever be tied to her. A nurse who nurtures life. A mother.

I've stalked her for two years, unable to stop but refusing to give in to the need to have her. To love her. Until the night her daughter is taken. I'll light up the world to get Leah's child back to her.

And then I'll walk away for good. Not because it's the right thing to do, but because I know how she'll look at me after seeing who I truly am.

She'll see the murderer inside me. And God help me, but she'll be right.

∞

Turn the page for an exclusive excerpt.

ASSASSIN'S HEART

Chapter One

Remi —

Brown sugar and butter melted on my tongue, bringing a groan to my lips as I waited in the gloomy garage. Abby's oatmeal molasses cookies. The vague memories of my mother baking when Levi, Eli, and I were children didn't include the flavors of finished cookies, but if the memories were heaven, oatmeal molasses cookies would have to be in there somewhere.

I took another bite.

I'd popped the last bit into my mouth when I caught sight of her. Fulton County Memorial needed actual fucking lighting in here to keep their employees safe, but even in the dim light I knew it was Leah coming out of the elevator onto the third floor of the parking garage. My Leah. Everything inside me stood up and took notice, like a live wire buzzing through my veins. Lighting up every nook and cranny of my body. That's what she did to me every. Damn. Time.

Shifting to ease the suddenly tight stretch of denim across my dick, I picked up another cookie. Leah walked toward an old Toyota Camry with a booster seat in the back. A reliable car for a woman who didn't make much despite her long hours and compassion. Compassionate people rarely earned what they deserved; it was the bastards like me that got ahead in this world. I waited for her to pull toward the down ramp, just out of sight, then shoved the rest of the cookie in my mouth, cranked my nondescript SUV, and followed.

Atlanta traffic was a bitch any time of day, but trying to get out of town in the evening... She'd have no chance to lose me, even if she knew I was behind her. Gridlock had us inching our way south, and from the way she rode her brakes, I knew she was as impatient as I to escape it. For far different reasons, but still. Her reason had blonde hair identical to hers, shades of yellow, caramel, and brown mingling together to provide a rich depth that made my fingers itch to touch it. Brown eyes just like hers too.

The child was six, I knew that. I knew her name and everything important about her, just like I did her mother. Not that either of them would ever know.

This far back, I couldn't catch a glimpse of those brown eyes in the rearview mirror. I wished I could. Every time I fucking saw her, I ached to stare into those eyes. They'd mesmerized me from the first moment I looked into them, drugged and disoriented from the coma, but Leah's dark eyes had stared down at me, grounded me, settled the fear in my gut.

There was nothing to settle the fear now, because that fear was reality—I'd never look into those eyes again. I would ache for her until I died, but I wouldn't give in. Leah and her child deserved a lot more in this life than a man with blood on his hands.

My cell rang as we exited the freeway at Union City. Leah's car headed west while I debated answering. I knew who was calling, and I knew he wouldn't be happy with me. He never was lately. Not that I gave a rat's ass, but I had no desire to waste time arguing.

I finally pressed the button on the console and answered. "Yeah?"

"Did the intel on our target pan out?"

No *hi, how are ya?* or even *how's it hanging, bro?* Levi was all business except on the rare occasions that his girlfriend, Abby, could trick him out of it. He'd raised me since I was ten, so I was used to it.

"It panned out," I told him. Butch Clarkson was definitely an abusive asshole. I didn't know who'd put a hit out on him, but he deserved everything he'd had coming his way. His wife was currently in a long-term care facility from a "fall down the stairs" that hadn't been an accident after all.

"Fine. Eli will start tracking his movements so we can—"

"Don't bother."

The silence that followed my words was heavy. Tense. Angry. And didn't faze me in the slightest.

"Why shouldn't I bother, Remi?"

"Because I took care of it." Clarkson would never throw another woman down the stairs. His associates wouldn't care, but I did.

Curses filtered through the speakers of the SUV. I barely paid attention, more interested in the little red Camry slowing ahead to turn into a neighborhood that was showing its age. The houses were a long commute from her work, smaller, with a bit more yard than new construction, but solid. Leah chose wisely, on a lot of things.

"I don't trust promises from men like you."

"Why the fuck would you do a job without full intel and without backup?" Levi growled, pulling me back from memories I should've buried a long time ago. "Are you trying to get yourself killed?"

The thought didn't bother me as much as it should have—a warning sign in my business. I brushed it off with a mental shrug. "I saw an opportunity and I took it. I knew all I needed to know."

"What I know is you have a fucking death wish. You're taking too many chances, Remi. You know better than that. *I taught you better than that.*"

You taught me a lot of things, big brother. Unfortunately lessons couldn't make you feel when all you wanted was to stop feeling.

I slowed, taking the same turn Leah had taken, far enough behind that she wouldn't notice. When she left the main road that bisected the neighborhood, I turned off my headlights and followed.

"This has got to stop, Remi."

Levi's words jerked me out of the fantasy of belonging in this little neighborhood with a woman and a little girl who deserved far better than me. He was right, too; he had no idea how right.

"You're risking too much and you know it. I can't lose you, brother. Either you rein it in or—"

"Or what?"

My words were deadly quiet. I could feel Levi's shock in the silence after them, knew he understood what I was saying—there was nothing he could do to stop me. I worked with my brothers because I wanted to, not because it was necessary.

The silence ticked by with the passing of car after car parked in front of each square of idealized domesticity. Levi finally spoke.

"Look, I love you; you know that. I even understand where you are coming from."

Because he knew about Leah. Or rather, about a woman; he didn't know her identity.

His voice went from gruff to dark and deadly, much as mine had been moments before. "But Remi, if you don't curb yourself, if you put Eli and Abby in danger, I will take care of business, don't you doubt it. I won't want to, but I will."

I didn't doubt it one bit. Levi would storm through hell to keep his woman safe. I knew because I felt the same. "Noted."

I clicked to end the call before either one of us could say something we really would regret—or before Levi could. I'd gone far beyond regret even before I took care of Mr. Wife Beater Clarkson.

Leah had parked in the driveway of a small gray house with weathered white trim. I pulled into a spot in front of a house catty-corner to hers, at just the right angle that I could see her fumbling to gather her things and get out of her car. I could see her walking up the sidewalk, her curves pulling my gaze down her body as she moved. I could see her sidestep to avoid the crack at the turn in the pavement just before the steps up to her porch. I didn't need to see any of it—I had watched her so many times that I knew each move by heart—yet I couldn't tear my eyes away.

And because I was watching, because I knew her body language better than my own, I saw the moment she hesitated outside the front entrance. Saw her keys fall from her hand to patter on the concrete before she yanked on the screen door.

Something wasn't right.

I was out of my car and crossing the street, heart pounding to the rhythm of my running feet, without a moment's hesitation. Leah's name escaped my lips over and over again, a mantra against the jacked-up fear I couldn't escape, no matter how irrational. It had been a single moment, one fleeting glimpse, but something inside me—instinct, paranoia, I didn't know what—said this wasn't irrational at all.

Put me in front of a gun with a round in the chamber and a finger on the trigger and my breath wouldn't even hitch. But Leah in danger? There was plenty of hitching. And swearing. And pleading with whatever spirit ruled the universe to keep her safe when I saw the broken-off knob on her screen door and the deep white gouges scarring the inner door's wood.

Someone had broken in—with Leah's child inside.

"Leah!"

Inside, chaos reigned though the room was empty. Furniture was out of place—the couch cushions split open, the coffee table overturned, the TV on its back as if its cabinet had been shoved. Toys and books and throw pillows were scattered among glass from a broken lamp and a tea cup and plate shattered into pieces. Every drawer, every door was open as if someone had been searching for something.

I took it all in with one sweeping glance as I struggled toward the kitchen to the left. "Leah!"

The kitchen was empty as well, the destruction in the front room repeated here. A tornado had torn through the house, but still, I saw no sign of the people who lived here.

Until a startled scream came from one of the back rooms.

I cursed, stretching my long legs as far as they would go, taking the hallway like a sprinter with the finish line in sight. I hit the back bedroom in time to see Leah kneeling beside an older woman on the floor next to a heavy dresser. The angle of the woman's neck told me all I needed to know, but Leah couldn't read the story—one shaking hand was reaching to find a pulse.

I snatched her back before her fingers could make contact.

Chapter Two

Leah —

The hard hands grabbing me sent a jolt of terror through my already trembling body. Before I could spin around, an arm slammed across my ribs and I was jerked back against a strong, muscular chest. Strength like that couldn't be escaped—my father had taught me that. *Best way to defeat your attacker, Leah girl; just don't let him get his hands on you in the first place.*

Too bad I hadn't paid attention to my six. That didn't mean I wouldn't fight.

Nails. Heels. Fists. I threw everything I had—for nothing. This guy was like a brick wall, unmoving. The thought of the same hands on my daughter, of what they'd done to Lydia, only sent my panic higher. And then a hand clamped onto my mouth, too wide to bite, and the brush of stubble against the side of my neck threatened to undo me.

"Stop right now, Leah. You hear me? Be still and listen."

Oh God.

I squeezed my eyelids shut tight. It couldn't be. I'd imagined that voice too many times to count in the past year and a half, that same hot, heavy tone. It haunted me, that voice. Why would it be here now?

I'd gone still without meaning to—shock had a way of doing that. It allowed Remi to get a better grip on me, to drag me back from Lydia's body. And it was a body; I could see that now, see what my heart hadn't wanted to accept when I'd stepped into the room. None of the spirit that had made the woman a perfect partner in raising Brooke was present in the limp flesh lying on the floor. The angle of her head told the nurse in me that her neck was broken, likely from a fall against the secondhand dresser I'd found in a consignment shop—old, heavy.

My mind understood what it was seeing, but my heart... God, my heart hurt so much.

Where was Brooke? If something had happened to her in the fight, she'd be here, right? They wouldn't have taken her body...

The thought of my six-year-old as *a body* sent a sob into the hand over my mouth. Remi's arms gentled, molding me almost tenderly to that immovable chest despite the fact that he didn't let me go. That softness was nearly as dangerous as the force he'd used to begin with. Dangerous enough to break me.

I jerked my legs, the only part of me that was free, off the ground and kicked them back, bending my knees sharply. The toes of my shoes barely brushed his crotch before Remi spun me toward the blank wall beside the dresser. My face planted against the pale yellow paint, I struggled to breathe with the full weight of two hundred and fifty pounds of sheer muscle pressing me forward. A hard thigh slid between mine—

"For your protection and mine, Leah," he said.

But the rough, raw quality to his words and the surge of pleasure between my legs told another story.

I beat my forehead against the wall, and the pleasure faded. This wasn't the man I'd fantasized about in the bed across the room. This wasn't a romantic…whatever my libido was trying to imagine it was. Lydia was dead. Brooke was missing. It was sick to be thinking about anything else right now.

"I'm going to move my hand so you can talk, okay?" Remi said in my ear. He sounded strong, in control. Resentment sparked in my stomach, burning hot. I'd been under men's control before, and it never worked out well for me. But tonight I had to think about Brooke.

I nodded.

Remi removed his hand, his fingers sliding across lips, cheek, jaw, and came to rest around my throat. Only slightly less threatening than before. I opened my mouth to point that out.

"Be careful," he warned me. "Be very careful, Leah."

So maybe not as in control as I'd thought. I had to swallow hard against the fear threatening to steal my voice. "Why?"

"Because I want to help you." He shifted behind me, and a heavy length pushing at the base of my spine flared into my awareness. "I can't to do that if you keep making trouble."

His words distracted me from his erection. "Why would you want to help me? Why are you even here?" I sucked in a deep, sudden breath, so sudden I choked. "You're a part of this, is that it? They left you here to confront me?" I jerked uselessly against his weight. "Where is my daughter?"

I felt more than saw his head shake. "I don't know where Brooke is. I'm not a part of this."

I attempted to throw a look over my shoulder, but the way he held me left no room to maneuver. "Why else would you be here?"

Remi took a deep breath, the expansion of his chest cutting off my air. On the exhale he eased back. "I'm not part of this. I can help you."

"You keep saying that." I peeled myself from the wall and turned just as carefully as he'd moved. "I'm not hearing another explanation."

Remi stood a few feet back, his arms locked over his chest, expression unreadable. This wasn't the man from my fantasies, the gruff but tender man I'd known for such a short time when he'd been injured. This man was hard. Cold. Dangerous.

I reached for my cell in my back pocket.

Remi watched, his gaze showing zero satisfaction when I found my pocket empty. He held up a hand— and my cell phone.

I reached for it. "I need to call the police, Remi."

He shook his head, keeping the phone just out of my reach. "She is beyond needing an ambulance and you know it," he said, jerking his chin toward Lydia. "The red tape cops would bring with them will only make it harder to find Brooke."

I forced my breath to stay even, my body still as my child's name left his lips. I hadn't spoken it aloud; I knew that. But Remi... "The only way you'd know her name was if you were involved. If you're not, give me the phone."

"I'm not involved."

"Then give me my phone. Now."

He slid the small black rectangle into his pocket. I lunged for it.

The next thing I knew, my hands were gripped in one of his and my jaw was in the other. He dragged me onto my tiptoes until I was almost level with him. "I'm not involved with whatever happened here," he bit out. "I promise."

I kneed him in the groin. Or tried to. Remi was prepared for everything, it seemed.

Fuck polite. Fuck complying with him—I went as crazy as I could with my hands in an unbreakable grip. Remi didn't take it lying down, but he didn't hurt me. Nor did he release my hands.

"Look," he barked, getting right in my face. "I don't know where Brooke is. I didn't take her. I don't know what the fuck is going on here—but I can't help you figure it out if you don't stop."

"It doesn't matter how many times you say it," I barked right back. "I don't believe you!"

Dragging me hard against him, he leaned in until his lips brushed mine and his golden-brown eyes were the only thing I could see. "I couldn't have done this because I wasn't here—I was following you home."

Following... "What?"

He released me, practically throwing my hands away. "I was following you from work. I came into the house after you. I couldn't have done this."

But my adrenaline-saturated brain wasn't getting it. "You followed me. From work?" I realized I was rubbing my aching wrists and forced myself to stop. *No sign of weakness.* "Why? How?" I shook my head hard. "How long have you been following me?"

"Long enough to know your daughter's name is Brooke. To know everything there is to know about her and you. What I don't know is who took her. At least not yet."

My stomach lurched, probably for a number of reasons—adrenaline, fear, confusion, and the sick certainty that my daughter was out there somewhere with someone who didn't care about her, someone who might hurt her. Someone who could disappear with her, and I would never see her again.

I barely made it to the hall bathroom before I threw up.

"Leah—"

"Out!" I shrieked. Surprisingly Remi retreated to the hall, giving me a few moments of semi-privacy to clean up the mess I'd made.

It wasn't until I began a quiet search of the cabinet for anything I could use as a weapon that he reappeared. "Not a good idea."

I allowed myself a moment to slump against the counter before straightening. "You're not going to convince me that you're a good guy, Remi. I've met your family, remember? They kidnapped me. You are fully capable of kidnapping a child. Just tell me where Brooke is and I'll do whatever you want."

A tick in his jaw was the only sign that what I'd just said might make him feel something, anything. Whatever it was, he fought it back. "I'm not going to waste time arguing with you anymore. You need to pack a bag."

"Why?"

"Because you can't stay here."

I threw up my hands. "And where do you suggest I go?" Not that I was going anywhere, especially with him. Brooke had been taken from here. I needed to be here in case her kidnappers came back. "I need to call the police, get them looking for her. I need to find her."

Remi grabbed the doorjamb on either side, the position both blocking my path and emphasizing the obscene size of his biceps and pecs. I forced my eyes to stay on his face, to stare him down no matter how much my insides felt like Jell-O.

"You already know what's happened to her, don't you?" he mused.

"I don't." And I didn't, not specifics anyway. That didn't mean I had no clue who was behind it. Hadn't feared something like this for years. I'd gotten complacent, though, allowed my guard down. Too soon, it seemed.

"You do," he said again, eyes narrowing when I tightened my lips. "You don't have to stay here, Leah. Whoever this is, they know how to get in touch with you. They will, when they're ready. Won't they?"

"And in the meantime?" I asked, ignoring his question. What was happening to my baby while they decided when they'd "be ready"?

"In the meantime—"

The ring of a phone cut Remi off, the sound originating from his pocket. Glancing from me to it, he fished the cell from his jeans and lifted it so I could see the white UNKNOWN flashing on the black screen. I reached for the phone.

"I don't think so," Remi said, pulling back just in time for my fingers to barely brush the edge. Turning the phone to himself, he clicked to answer the call, then clicked Speaker.

And waited.

"Leah?"

My heart slammed into my ribs. I staggered back to sit on the closed toilet seat, gripping the edges like they could keep me upright and sane—except I didn't think that was possible. Not anymore.

Chapter Three

Remi —

I narrowed my eyes on Leah's face, watching the color leach out, the way her hands came up, almost as if to ward something—or someone—off. She knew that voice. It scared her. Why?

"Who is this?" I used the tone that made marks shit their pants.

Silence. I could practically hear the man calculating, deciding on the best course of action. What I didn't hear was backing down.

"Oh, Leah," the man finally said. "You know better than to bring someone else into this."

"Where is Brooke?" she asked, voice trembling as much as her body. I could see it, see the fear gripping her. The need to pull her close, to comfort her, give her the safety of my arms, rose to choke me, but I forced it ruthlessly away. Now wasn't the time, nor would Leah welcome my touch.

"Brooke is safe," the man said. "Did you have any doubt?"

"You killed Lydia," she said, her tone all *hell yeah I doubt it.*

A heavy sigh crossed the line. He got her message loud and clear. He could read her just by her voice.

He knew her. Intimately. The thought blazed through my mind, hazing everything in red.

"An unfortunate accident," he was saying. "I didn't let Brooke see, I assure you of that. She is safe and sound."

"I want to speak to her," Leah said. "Please. Just let me tell her it's okay."

The little sob that said everything definitely wasn't okay tore at me, threatened to distract me even more than the jealousy. I'd never encountered that before—on a job I was all business; emotion wasn't a factor.

With Leah it was all emotion. Definite distraction.

"I always knew you'd be a wonderful mother," the man said. "But right now I don't think speaking to Brooke is the best idea. She's finally calm. Hearing Mommy's voice would undo all my hard work."

Hectic color hit Leah's cheeks. "You're a bastard."

"I'm not, Leah. You know I'm not."

A tear squeezed out as she closed her eyes, tearing at my gut, but there was no trace of weakness when she asked, "How did you find us?"

"An informant. He'd seen a news story a while ago, something about you being kidnapped?" Concern creeped in, making my skin crawl. "Everything turned out fine, it seems."

Leah scoffed. "Would you care if it hadn't?"

"How could you even ask me that?"

Leah tightened her lips in that way she had when she desperately wanted to say something but shouldn't. She knew him as well as he did her, then.

How well?

I shoved the question down deep. The caller was keeping this personal; getting down to business might throw him off. "What is it you want?" I asked.

Another pause—he didn't like talking to me. It proved my point. Finally he spoke, his tone almost tired. "Leah knows what I want; I'm sure she'll fill you in. She returns what belongs to a certain powerful someone, and she gets what belongs to her back safe and sound. That's it. Simple." Another sigh. "I'll be waiting, Leah."

The call clicked off.

As if her strings had been cut, Leah dropped to her knees on the floor, her body bowing down over her thighs. No matter how much my brain shouted that it was a bad idea, my heart forced me to go to her. Sobs threatened to choke her as she rocked forward and back, her face practically on the floor, crying her daughter's name—I couldn't stand it, couldn't leave her in so much fucking pain that it was ripping *my* guts out.

Kneeling down, I planted my knees on either side of hers and pulled her up into my arms, her face in the hollow of my shoulder, her tears soaking my shirt.

Holy shit.

I knelt there, her soft, trembling body against mine, and knew, in that moment, that I was lost. I had long ago decided never to walk back into her life. I could never be what she needed, except right now I actually was. Everything she needed.

I couldn't walk away from that.

And some damned part of me, down deep where I'd buried it alongside those memories of family and love and peace, was fucking ecstatic. I was holding the woman I loved in my arms for the very first time.

While she cried for her missing child.

Christ, I was a bastard.

The knowledge made my voice rougher than I wanted. "We need to go."

Leah shook her head against my chest.

I eased back, tilted her chin up until those liquid brown eyes met mine. "We need to go."

She blinked, still hazy. A pair of tears rolled down her cheeks.

I don't know what I was thinking; hell, maybe I wasn't thinking at all. I'd thought my instincts were all for killing, not for caring. But something I couldn't resist pushed me forward until my lips trapped a tear against her skin. My tongue snaked out to brush it away, to take the taste of her pain into my mouth. I moved to the other side and traced the path of her tears from jaw to eye, her lashes fluttering against my skin. When I straightened, so did she.

Our lips barely brushed each other.

Something powerful, something holy clenched my heart into a fucking knot behind my too-tight ribs.

"Leah"—I grabbed her arms and moved her away from me, telling myself I wasn't tearing a piece of me out while doing it—"we need to go." I made myself breathe, focus. "We can't find her tonight." At least not from here. Back home I had what I needed to get us started.

Leah looked anywhere but at me. Was she angry? Disgusted?

Did it matter?

"I can't—"

"You can." Pushing myself to my feet, I dragged her up with me. "What is it he wants? Is it here?" I doubted it considering the state of the house. Leah wouldn't keep something here that might draw danger to her daughter.

When she didn't answer, I gave her a little shake. "Is it?"

Making a visible effort to pull herself together, she wiped the backs of her hands across her eyes, smearing mascara as she went. She looked like she had been through hell and back—and she had—and still I had a hard time believing any woman could be so beautiful.

Would you get your mind on now and not your dick?

I dropped my hands. "Leah?"

Fists clenched at her side. She lifted her head to glare at me. "Go to hell, Remi."

I wanted to hear my full name on her lips—not the shortened version, but the whole thing, just once. I wanted her to say it when we were as close as we'd been moments ago. To say it when I was inside her. I wanted—

To hell with what I wanted. *Bastard, remember? Be the bastard you both need you to be.*

"I'm all you've got right now, so if I'm going to hell, you better pack for warm weather."

"I'm not leaving."

I raised an eyebrow. "You want to stay here with Mrs. Lydia?"

The words drained the fight from Leah's body—exactly what I'd hoped to accomplish. The stricken look on her face made me wish I could kick my own ass.

I forced my own anger out with a deep breath. "Look, I don't have anything here that can help you. I need you to come with me." I held up the phone. "They obviously know how to contact you."

She reached for the phone, and I slipped it back into my pocket. If she got ahold of it, I'd probably never see her again. At least if she had a say in it.

Which she didn't. Not right now.

She stared at the pocket where I'd tucked away her lifeline to her daughter. White teeth gleamed as she began to nibble at her bottom lip. I forced back a groan. Apparently it didn't matter what the situation was; anything Leah did made me tight and aching. All I could do was try to ignore it

"Do you have family you can contact?" I asked reluctantly. Brooke's father wasn't still in the picture, I knew that much—after over a year of watching, I'd never seen a sign of any man in Leah's life, thank fuck. I might've lost my shit long before now if I had.

Was he somehow involved with this?

I pushed the thought aside to examine later. "Do you have *anyone* you can contact who can help you like I can?"

Her dark eyes snapped to meet mine. "I can't get past the fact that I haven't seen you for a year and a half, Remi, and on the night my daughter is kidnapped, you miraculously reappear."

I shrugged. "Just because you haven't seen me doesn't mean I haven't seen you."

"Don't remind me. You're definitely not helping your case." She brought her hands up to rub her temples. "You have to be involved with this. There's no other logical explanation."

The words were weak, though, without the biting sting Leah could add when you pissed her off. She was holding on to the idea because it gave her some knowledge, some control in the midst of a confusing, chaotic world. I recognized the signs and couldn't blame her. She could hang on to whatever she needed to—as long as she came with me.

"Well"—I stepped aside, raised a hand to usher her toward the hallway—"if I'm involved, you'd better stick to me like glue. What better way to find your daughter?"

She stared me down a moment longer, brown eyes wary. And worried. When they dropped to the ground and she moved toward me, I knew I had won.

"All right," she said. "For now."

∞

Grab your copy of ASSASSIN'S HEART today!

"Ms. Sheridan writes suspense that grabs you and won't let go."

~ *Tea and Book*

About the Author

Ella Sheridan never fails to take her readers to the dark edges of love and back again. Strong heroines are her signature, and her heroes span the gamut from hot rock stars to alpha bodyguards and everywhere in between. Ella never pulls her punches, and her unique combination of raw emotion, hot sex, and action leave her readers panting for the next release.

Born and raised in the Deep South, Ella writes romantic suspense, erotic romance, and hot BDSM contemporaries. Start anywhere—every book may be read as a standalone, or begin with book one in any series and watch the ties between the characters grow.

Connect with Ella at:

Ella's Website – ellasheridanauthor.com
Facebook – Ella Sheridan: Books and News
Twitter – @AuthorESheridan
Instagram – @AuthorESheridan
Pinterest – @AuthorESheridan
Bookbub – Ella Sheridan
E-mail – ella@ellasheridanauthor.com

∞

For news on Ella's new releases, free book opportunities, and more, sign up for Ella's newsletter at ellasheridanauthor.com .

Ella Sheridan